# A SILENCE
# OF DESIRE

A novel by KAMALA MARKANDAYA
Author of *Nectar in a Sieve*
and *Some Inner Fury*

How men and women embroil themselves
and each other by silence at the wrong times,
by exchanging only surface thoughts when
their need is to unburden their hearts, is the
universal theme of this novel.

The story of a few critical months in a
hitherto serene marriage, it is set in present-
day India. Dandekar is a government clerk
who lives a comfortable and well ordered life
with his wife and children. But when he finds
Sarojini not at home to get his dinner on
several occasions, his suspicions of her are
readily aroused, and they are as good as confirmed by his chance discovery of a strange
man's photograph in the family trunk.
Shocked and incredulous, Dandekar finds
himself caught in the beginnings of a web
of concealment which he himself is soon
helping to spin.

Involved in the web eventually are not
only Dandekar and Sarojini, but also her med-
dlesome Cousin Rajam, Dandekar's office
colleagues and superiors, and above all a
swami who has earned the devotion of some
and the persecution of others as a faith healer.

In weaving this absorbir
bringing Dandekar finally t
destiny, Kamala Markanday
a master of plot and charact
*Nectar in a Sieve* and *Some*

# A SILENCE OF DESIRE

NOVELS BY

## Kamala Markandaya

\*

A SILENCE OF DESIRE

SOME INNER FURY

NECTAR IN A SIEVE

Kamala Markandaya

# A SILENCE
# OF DESIRE

The John Day Company
New York

© 1960 BY KAMALA MARKANDAYA

Library of Congress Catalogue
Card Number: 60-11299

MANUFACTURED IN THE UNITED STATES OF AMERICA

# A SILENCE OF DESIRE

# 1

THE six rooms that they rented were built around a courtyard, a square of about eight feet with an uneven cement floor in the middle of which stood the divine tulasi that his wife worshiped. It was a small evergreen plant, crammed into bright and decorative brass in which it languished, surviving without health, but with a sharp, imperious smell that made you forget its looks—a smell that clung to your hands until you had washed and scrubbed, and even after, and could haunt you if you did not pray. Dandekar did not pray to it, he was always careful to say; it was a plant—one did not worship plants—but it was a symbol of God, whom one worshiped, and it was necessary that God should have symbols, since no man had the power or temerity to visualize him.

Dandekar often made this point in the office where he worked, where some of the clerks were Indian Christians,

converts, zealous to mark the difference between the worship of God, and idolatory. Cows, snakes, plants, ranked
as idols; paintings, prints and statues did not. It incensed
Dandekar. He had been at pains to bring up his children
with a correct understanding of these matters, and to edu-
cate his wife. Not that she did not understand; her religious tutelage had been rather more earnest than his own,
and she often had answers to conundrums which his less
amiable, non-Hindu friends set him—not, of course, that
she would supply them until he had indicated that, perhaps, she might. So it was not that she did not understand;
it was just that sometimes she seemed to forget, tending
the tulasi with a reverence which it did not merit. And
yet, he had to concede, it was a fine point, the difference
between the reverence due to a symbol and to its actual-
ity; between the tulasi tree and its Maker. Still, sometimes
she went too far.

Overhead was the patch of bright blue sky which you
could see from here, the courtyard, but from none of the
rooms in any of the flats except the topmost one. His eye
traveled up the eight stories of the building. He knew
them all intimately; he and his wife, and later his children,
had lived in each of them in turn, graduating slowly
downwards to the luxury of the ground floor, the courtyard, and first call on the tap mounted on a pedestal in one
corner. The other tenants used it too, but at the convenience of the Dandekars, not their own. Yes, they had pros-

pered. Three children, no debts, a steady job, a fair pile
of savings that his wife regularly and methodically converted into gold—bangles, a necklace, earrings and
brooches—less for ornamentation than the security it rep-
resented. Gold was stable. It might have surprised the
Dandekars to learn that a fairly extensive organization existed to stabilize this precious commodity, but they would
have approved. On what else should townspeople rely?
Land was certainly the preferable alternative, but land in
town was too dear to buy. Once, when he was newly
married, very foolish, very young, Dandekar had spoken
to his still-younger wife of owning the building they lived
in; but not since. He had become a realist. Sarojini had
been a realist, even then. She had spoken wistfully of the
seventh floor, one floor below them, and the heaven of
carrying water up one flight less of stairs. Well, she did no
more fetching and carrying now. He was a senior clerk
and they employed a servant girl, and it gave him real and
considerable pleasure to think he could do as much for his
wife.

She was a good wife, Sarojini: good with the children,
an excellent cook, an efficient manager of his household, a
woman who still gave him pleasure after fifteen years of
marriage, less from the warmth of her response than from
her unfailing acquiescence to his demands. He was lucky
there, he knew from guarded, half-revelatory conversations with his colleagues. Other men's wives thought of

the working day ahead, or of the possibility of yet another baby, feigned sleep, pleaded malady, practiced one or another of those little coldnesses which emasculated a man as effectively as any more ruthless method. Sarojini came to him when he wanted her, placidly; but since she had never done otherwise he did not miss the passion. She did most things placidly, he thought with affection; and from this calm proceeded the routine and the regularity that met the neat and orderly needs of his nature.

For instance, now that she had heard his step in the courtyard she would be putting the potatoes in to fry. The agreeable hiss would last until he had washed and changed, and by then she would be ready for him, and so would the evening meal. He was always ready for it; it was a long gap from midday lunch to seven o'clock supper, with nothing in between but a cup of watery coffee that the peon brought in from the coffee shop next door.

At the thought of eating, his stomach began to heave; it was a pleasant sensation, providing, he thought in passing, one was certain of food. Kicking off his sandals he walked briskly to the tap, washed meticulously hands, face, feet, rinsed the taste of dust from his mouth, and went in to change. It was while he was winding his dhoti around him that he realized something was missing. There was no sound from the kitchen. A pity, he thought. He had never formulated it in words, but his wife's move-

ments, the noises of cooking, were part of his homecoming.

He finished tying his dhoti, smoothed back his wet hair,
went out once more into the courtyard, for none of the
rooms intercommunicated, and so to the kitchen. It was
empty.

Somewhere in the building he could hear the voices of
his two daughters, squabbling. Doubtless on the terrace;
it was their favorite rendezvous, as it was, it seemed to
him, of half the children in the neighborhood. He called
without hope and was not answered. He shouted for the
maidservant and she came, a wizened girl of fifteen or so,
carrying his youngest child, drowsy and irritable, strad-
dled across her hip. He raised his voice above the fretful
whining.

"Where is your mistress?"

The maid giggled. It was a habit with her, pleasing or
maddening according to the moment.

"Mistress gone out."

"Gone out. I can see she has gone out. Where?"

"Mistress not say." Again the irritating giggle. "Telling
me look after Chandru-baba and gone out."

"What time did she go?"

In answer the girl rolled her eyes, checking the giggle in
deference to the thunder in Dandekar's face. He recalled
that she did not know how to tell the time. She was an

utter fool. She did not know anything. He vented his rising ill-humor on her.

"And is this the way to look after Chandru-baba? He should have been asleep long ago. Mistress leaves you in charge just for one evening and you cannot even get the child to sleep. See how tired he is!—naturally, being carried about at this hour."

"Chandru-baba giving trouble, sir. Calling his mother, crying to lie down. Not my fault, sir." Now there were two of them whining.

"Be quiet, or you will wake him up fully." He spoke more fiercely than he intended, mainly from alarm at the thought of being saddled with a crying child for the best part of the night. "Be quiet, do you hear?" But the girl's whimpers became sobs; she was a little alarmed too, for the same reason.

"Not my fault, sir." She gulped and the tears ran faster as she struggled to hold the kicking, screaming child and at the same time to wipe her wet and, he thought, singularly foolish face. He stared at her, feeling helpless and angry, afraid to say anything more in case he provoked another appalling outburst, and wondering what tiresome dispensation of Providence it was that made it so easy for women to weep.

It was on this unquiet scene that Sarojini came in.

The child's cries, halted in mid-scream at her approach, began again on a milder note and were finally hushed as she took him in her arms. The servant girl's sobs ceased. Dandekar handed over to his wife with relief.

In half an hour's time order was restored. Chandru was asleep. The maid was invisible, which was what Dandekar most desired she should be. Sarojini was getting him his meal, frying rice in a little butter, stirring saffron and cori- ander into the potato mixture.

"It won't be long." Sarojini spoke encouragingly to her husband. "You see I left everything ready . . . there is only the um . . ." She moved deftly up and down the small room, assembling a dozen different cups on a tray in between giving a stir to the pots on the fire. ". . . only the crisping to do now, which could not be done before."

"But where did you go at such an awkward time?" Dandekar's voice was sour. Relief at her return had ob- scured other issues, now the sense of grievance crept back.

"It was an awkward time." Sarojini busied herself fill- ing the cups on the tray. "But you know what people are, they do not always think of your convenience, and when my cousin called—"

"Which cousin?"

"Cousin Rajam. I could not send her away in time."

Dandekar chuckled. "Who can? How that woman talks! But where did you go with her?"

"Only as far as the bus stop. She could not remember where it was."

"And she has been here fifty times . . . though it does not take you an hour to walk from there to here, does it? Why, it's not a quarter of a mile!" He was grumbling again, recalling the fearful time he had spent.

"We had to wait for a bus." Sarojini did whatever was to be done swiftly, and picked up the tray. "Dinner is ready."

He followed her into the cramped dining room, where two places were laid—smooth wooden planks on which to sit, and fresh green plantain leaves on which Sarojini was arranging the cups. This room always made Dandekar feel at ease. It did not seem to him to be cramped, except on festal occasions when relations came, and then he blamed the crowd. He hardly ever noticed that the walls were yellowed and greasy from cooking fumes, which easily surmounted the four-foot partition between the kitchen and dining room, and anyway most of the wall space was taken up by framed prints. These were all of gods and goddesses, singly and in groups, tableaux that showed them holding court in their heavens, or warring, or being miraculously born of the earth or the sea. He liked these colored pictures, even if he could not have described a single one of them in detail; they were part of his wife's and his own background, familiar and reassuring.

Sarojini was serving. Dandekar eased himself down on to his plank, neatly crossed his legs, and as part of the evening ritual began shouting for his daughters. Then he realized no places had been laid for them, and he stopped.

"The girls," he said, "have they eaten already?"

"Yes. That is to say, no," said Sarojini. "I gave them money to buy tiffin . . . they will not want anything more."

"Money for tiffin," repeated Dandekar. "It seems as if you knew you would have to wait so long for a bus!"

"Oh no," said Sarojini quickly. "It's just that—well, you know what girls are, they like to have tiffin outside sometimes, it makes a change from home cooking."

"A change that I would never seek," said Dandekar, generously. He was feeling happier, back to normal. "You never know what ingredients these restaurants use, do you? The cheapest, certainly, they've got to make a profit, haven't they? Why, only today in the office Pillai was telling me—"

He began recounting the day's activities, a pursuit which gave him pleasure especially when, as now, his irreverent daughters were absent. Sarojini was unquestioning, and she was a good listener.

# 2

DANDEKAR usually walked to and from the office. This saved bus fares, which in a month amounted to very nearly six rupees. Six rupees, admittedly, was not a fortune; but, as Dandekar often said, there were better uses to which it could be put. What he did with it was, at the close of each month, to take a bus ride to the market at the other end of the town, and there to expend it on, first, rose water or some similar toilet preparation for his wife; second, a toy for the baby and trinkets for the girls; and finally, hulvas or sweets for general distribution. All these were in the nature of semiluxuries.

Dandekar seldom paused to analyze his pleasures. Nor was he of that ill-starred band that, no stranger to bitterness and sorrow, remarks each moment of peace, and is careful to say: *Now* I am happy. Dandekar did not bother. He was humming to himself as he got off the bus, and he stopped humming for the sole purpose of beating down the bangle man who was attempting to extract an exorbitant price for a pair of glass bangles for his daughter.

"A child's wrist," he said, "and you are asking as much as you would for a grown woman."

"Size makes no difference," answered the man. "Glass is cheap. The work is the same whether child's bangle or woman's."

It was the classic argument, gone over countless times by many bangle buyers and many bangle sellers. Dandekar raised his absolutely final offer. The man lowered his rock-bottom price. Dandekar was humming again as, his purchase completed, he wandered to the next booth. Here were the hulvas, translucent green and orange cubes studded with pistachios and almonds. Dandekar chose, haggled, bought, extracted and ate one glutinous cube from the newspaper cone which he had been handed. He was peacefully and fastidiously licking one sticky forefinger, one sticky thumb, when he heard his name called. The song died on his lips. He knew his wife's Cousin Rajam's voice.

"Cousin, Cousin Dandekar! What a nice surprise to see you here!"

He did not like her calling him Cousin. He was not her cousin, except by marriage. Was she then to address him as Cousin-by-marriage? No, he answered himself, there were other appellations. But he never had the courage to tell her so.

"Why should it be a surprise?" He turned to face her. "I come here—" He was about to say: "on the last day of each month," but then he panicked, in case she lay in wait for him, and changed it to "fairly frequently."

"Do you?" Rajam beamed at him. Here was a sunny disposition, tiring only those who liked a little shade with their sun. "So do I. How strange I have not come across you here before."

In fact it was not strange at all. Rajam drew her widow's pension on the first of each month, and by the end there was nothing left with which to go marketing. Dandekar's routine was the opposite. In the first weeks of the month the saved bus fares were accumulating, and it was not until the end that he had anything worth while to come to market with.

"And how are your lovely daughters?" Rajam forced the conversation along.

"Very well."

"The baby?"

"Very well."

"And—I should have asked first—dear Cousin Sarojini?"

"She is well too," said Dandekar, and he could not help adding, "Much the same as when you saw her last."

"It seems such ages ago," sighed Rajam. "How time does fly! The days just come and go, before you know where you are a whole year has gone."

She was, thought Dandekar, exaggerating unpardonably.

"A few days," he said dryly, "is hardly an age. I cannot even imagine that it seems so."

"A few days," repeated Rajam. "Who said it was a few days? More like six months—let me see now, it was just after the New Year, because I remember—"

She made her calculations, which yielded the result of four months. "Which—you can ask anyone—is a long time," she concluded, "and may well be reckoned an age."

"Four months," said Dandekar. "Are you sure?"

"Of course I'm sure," said Rajam. "Did you not hear me just now, working out the exact day of my last visit?"

Dandekar had not listened to these complications. He hardly listened to the rest of Rajam's conversation, and she, growing tired at last of his stony monosyllables, said that she must be going, and half an hour later went.

Dandekar rode back by bus, his pleasure in this monthly outing that he sanctioned himself unaccountably diminished. Rajam had made it amply clear that she was not wrong; well then, Sarojini must have made a mistake. That of course was the simple explanation and he must accept it, he told himself, and indeed to some extent he did so; but something remained, as troubling and elusive as minutest grit in the eye.

When he got home Sarojini, a little to his disappointment, was not in. It was his own fault; he had returned

earlier than usual, the desire to linger in the market having
been taken from him, what with Rajam and one thing
and another. He stood in the courtyard, wondering where
she could be and telling himself, reasonably, that a housewife was not physically chained to the house, yet feeling
somehow a little adrift. Within a few minutes, however,
he heard his wife's step, the slight swish of her sari, and he
brightened.

"Sarojini," he said.

She started, then recovered herself. "Why, it's you,"
she said. "How lovely—you're home early."

"Did I startle you? I'm sorry."

"Well yes, you did." She laughed. "But I shouldn't be
so jumpy at my age, should I? It's just that I didn't see you
at first, you were standing so still."

"I've got something for you." He moved toward her,
awkward with his parcels—women's things, fragile. "A
small present."

"Have you really?" There was real pleasure in her
voice, and either genuine surprise or a very good simula-
tion of it. It was one of her amiable qualities. She must
have known by now, since this was not the first time it
had happened, that he bought her something on the last
day of each month; yet she always managed to be pleasantly surprised.

The children, on the other hand, had grown to expect
it. Usually they were glued to the doorstep, waiting for

him to arrive; it was only today, being early, that he had beaten them to it. But soon, hearing voices, they came running in, pelting down the stairs that zigzagged up to the terrace, skirts and pigtails flying.

"What's the hurry?" He teased them. "Maybe you are late for an important appointment?"

He was very fond of his daughters, Lakshmi who was ten, her face still rounded in the contours of childhood, but lanky-limbed, and Ramabai, nearly twelve, who secretly longed to be a film star, and as a first step to this end nagged everyone to call her Rani, instead of her old-fashioned given name. She put both bangles on one wrist now, in the new way, instead of one on each as her mother did, and moved her hands gracefully, admiring the delicate glass.

"Does madam like it?"

"Oh yes." She smiled at him. "You see it goes so well with my skirt."

He did not think so. The bangle was yellow and blue, and her skirt was red and green. Then he noticed his wife was wearing the same colors, a green Mysore silk with a red border which he knew, more from association than any explicit recognition, was her temple sari. Whenever he saw her in it he usually searched around and eventually remembered whatever religious festival it was, but now after a good try he had to give up.

"I'd forgotten today was festival day," he said, tentatively, reluctant to ask directly and hoping his wife would give him a line.

"What festival?" asked Sarojini.

"Isn't it a festival?"

"No," said Sarojini. "Whatever made you think it was?"

"I don't know," he said. "It's just that, seeing you in that sari—"

"Oh that," she said. "I just decided it would do for everyday use. It's such an old thing it's not worth keeping for special occasions, I may as well wear it before it perishes."

Dandekar looked at the sari. It did not look near perishing to him. Mysore silks are hardy, and this one was not an exception. Of course it was old, but then the sari she wore to weddings was older still, and there was no question of converting that for everyday use.

"It looks nice enough to me," he contented himself with saying.

The girls, the presentation over, had gone back to their cronies, zigzagging up the stairs to the flat roof, bursting to exhibit their new acquisitions. Sarojini, the unstoppered bottle in her hand, was massaging a little sandal oil into her wrist, the back of her hand, the palm. He watched her, the delicate circling motions she made, the oil extending and gleaming on her pale skin.

"They say there is nothing to equal this oil for the

skin," she said. She sniffed appreciatively. "The smell is exquisite too."

"Is it? Yes, so it is." He recovered himself. "An excellent smell."

"My cousins used to say, if you used it all the time, you would never get a wrinkle."

"Did they?"

"Yes. But Uncle was a supervisor in the Government Sandal Oil Factory, if you remember, so they could easily afford—"

"Did you say Cousin Rajam?" He spoke almost without realizing.

"Cousin Rajam? No, I just said my cousins, the ones who used to live—"

"No, I mean before. You said she came to see you."

"When?"

"A few days ago. When you went to the bus stop with her."

"I said Pankajam. I said Cousin Pankajam, not Cousin Rajam."

"Oh, I see," he said with relief. "That explains it. I must have misheard you."

"It doesn't matter which cousin, does it?" she asked.

"No, no," he said hurriedly. "It's just that I happened to meet your Cousin Rajam in the market, and she said it was such a long time since she had seen you."

"Quite a long time," said Sarojini. "Let me see now, it was after the New Year—"

Not for the first time Dandekar listened as she threaded a tortuous way, as through a maze, to the correct date. Her system was similar to Rajam's and, indeed, common to all the women he knew. Contemptuous of calendar dates, as men were contemptuous of them for it, they used feast days, birthdays and their children's illnesses as steppingstones to arrive at the answer; and, infuriatingly, they were invariably right.

# 3

DANDEKAR did not think about it, and if asked he probably would not have admitted that, on the whole, he quite enjoyed working in an office. Muruges, the office boy, did not; he was going to be a painter, or so he said, and anything in between was a waste of his talents. Narayan did not. He was a B.A. with honors, a graduate of Madras University, deserving of better things than this junior clerkship which in frequent moments of truth he knew was the most he was ever likely to get. The rest of them had no great objection to working in the office— at least in this office. There were offices, they knew, where their friends worked, where the officers, put on their mettle by prophecies, during the last unkind days of the British raj, of forthcoming ineptitude, muddle and disaster, had instituted regimes of such efficiency and order that they indeed gave rise to feelings of inadequacy and guilt in their frail human underlings.

That it was different here, the atmosphere genial, was due in large measure to the head of the department, a weathered and brilliant ex-Congress leader, organizer, and now civil servant, who hid his long and awkward baptismal name under the convenient title of C. V. Chari —a name far enough removed from the anglicizations and simplifications of the old days as to pass muster with the most Indian Indian, and at the same time be acceptable to the English, as regrettably stiff-tongued as ever. Moreover —and Chari shuddered when he thought of it—it stopped Americans, of whom there were a good few these days in the new free India, from trying to pronounce his name. "Just call me C. V.," he would say blandly when (quite soon) they got to the stage of Christian names, and Americans, itching to get their tongues around Indian words, would courteously if reluctantly comply, vague thoughts of Clarences or Cuthberts, or their embarrassing Indian equivalents, floating through their minds.

Chari had been a member of the Indian Civil Service, that service which, according to the crisp contemporary description, was neither Indian, nor civil, nor of service, so that when at last the ugly imperialist interlude was over, one of the first actions of the new democracy was to rename its civil service, so important are brand and labels. He had got there by sheer worth, being one of the few Indians to be seconded directly into the Service without an English degree, or qualifications, or patronage. Indeed, he had never even been to England, though his knowledge of that country, from books, might well have chastened an Englishman.

Chari did not, even in those perfervid nationalistic days, either vociferously accept or refute the charges against the I.C.S. He watched, waited, and when further service would have meant screwing his conscience out of true, he resigned. After a further long period of waiting he joined the Congress Party where, more or less despite himself (he would have preferred to be happier in the humbler ranks), he was hauled to the forefront and leadership. A good deal of the next decade, consequently, he spent in jail; and when independence came these jail sentences stood him in good stead, nicely balancing the prejudice, in an intensely Indian India, against his former British liaison. Now he was an honored member of the Indian Administrative Service—praised where he had once been reviled, and confirmed in his opinion that he could survive both.

Dandekar's liking for Chari was strong, strong enough to withstand even the shock of learning that he had left his wife. Holding conformist views on marriage, any other man he would have condemned out of hand; but in Chari's case he had said, at the time, that he would like to hear his side of the story. This he would never do, for the wall between clerks and officers is high anywhere, even in democracies, and so Dandekar was spared the pain of passing sentence.

The subject was hardly ever raised now. It was three years old, stale, discussed dry at the time, with neither gossip nor rumors to keep it alive. If they talked about marriage now it was in general terms, with views that varied from Sastri's, who went to see films of Indian classical stories and held the benign belief that wives were faithful, virtuous creatures, prepared like their classical sisters to follow their husbands barefoot into the jungle, if necessary, to Joseph's, who believed in free love and was even said to practice it. There was a third view, a curious result of Western films, the strongest adherent of which was Mahadevan. He believed that no marriage was safe unless, in her husband's absences, a wife was locked in a chastity girdle. He was a bachelor.

"Our women are not like that," Dandekar remonstrated mildly. "They don't flaunt themselves in front of men, either before marriage or after. They're brought up differently."

"Times are changing," said Mahadevan. "There is divorce now—why should there be divorce unless there is infidelity?"

"By the man," suggested Dandekar, this being the lesser crime.

"With a woman," said Mahadevan. "And more than

likely a married woman—at least we are still careful with our girls. But even they, just see what sheep's eyes they make when they pass a student from the boys' college, and whispers and giggles!"

"That's human nature," said Dandekar tolerantly. He thought Mahadevan a bit of a fanatic.

"Yes, but human nature doesn't stop there," said Mahadevan, "otherwise you and I wouldn't be here. I'm not saying that our girls—I'm not saying that. They have no opportunity and we see to it that they haven't. But what about married women?"

"I'd guess you were not married even if I didn't know," said Dandekar leniently. "Married women may have the opportunity, but where have they the time? Morning till evening there is something to do, and children hanging around them all day wanting this and that done."

This was more than he would have admitted had Sarojini been present. It was also something he had not believed until two years ago when his wife fell ill, and by malevolent mischance, simultaneously, all their female relatives fell ill, and he had had to manage on his own.

"Oh well, you're a married man, you should know." Mahadevan dismissed the subject, hearing in the distance the thunder that indicated that coffee was about to be served.

Kannan, the peon, created this thunder partly because he used a large biscuit-can lid to carry the brass cups of coffee, partly because he was not too steady, these days, on his feet. Dandekar often thought that if he were Kannan he would get a proper tray, instead of this flimsy tin that bucked and bent so deafeningly when you carried it, if it meant appealing to Chari himself. But Kannan had a very good reason, in that he had on three separate occasions appropriated the money Chari had given him for the purpose; and the noise did not trouble him. He had a rag to mop up the slopped coffee and—after all, the tin lid did as well as any. He wiped the lid now, and the undersides of the dripping cups, before setting them down on the unpolished table. Dandekar averted his eyes from the disreputable rag, being used to his wife's cleanly ways. Mahadevan, living in bachelor quarters, had developed no such fads; he drank his coffee as he ate his food, with an enjoyment untempered by finicky thoughts as to how it was cooked or served. In a way Dandekar envied him; it must simplify life to have so few qualms, but he would not have changed places with him.

Coffee came between ten and twelve in the mornings and two and four in the afternoons, depending on the vagaries of the temperamental Brahmin cook in the coffee shop. These were the highlights of the day, for with the coffee went a quarter of an hour's break.

"A legacy from the British," said Sastri, giving credit where credit was due, not for the first time. "You see they did leave some good things behind them."

"It is a fallacy in your thinking," said Narayan, embittered because his talents were rotting here in this humdrum office, and tracing culpability back to the years of occupation, which were echoes from his childhood and never really known. "Do you think if the British hadn't come we wouldn't have thought of it? Do you think in the past people worked on and on and on right through the day until the British arrived and told them to stop for a cup of tea?"

They were silenced. None of them knew what their ancestors had done, three centuries ago.

"The British have told us many a time of all they have done," continued Narayan. He sneered. "They built railways, roads, bridges. Do you think in Russia, China, Japan, where there were no British, there are no roads, railways, bridges? Do you think—"

Dandekar pondered. They had been taught that, of course. He still had in his possession one of his school textbooks, in which, following the historical outlines of each Indian province, had come a chapter entitled "Benefits of British Rule." He remembered it very clearly, because they had had to memorize the contents, and roads, railways, bridges, had certainly figured prominently. At this point he realized, uneasily, that he had been thinking recently of getting this very same book out of the tin trunk in which it had lain all these years, and giving it to his younger daughter. Now he saw that that must never be done; it would be teaching a child untruth. Was it un-truth? The British *had* built roads, railways, bridges; but if they hadn't somebody else would have, whoever had come instead of the British, and then it would have been a benefit of *their* rule. But if they hadn't come? Here growing a little confused, he shelved the issue, though he still felt that it was not the kind of book to hand to a child.

Usually with Dandekar if he was thinking of doing something it took him weeks or even months. He recognized this weakness in himself however, and therefore if there was something he felt he really ought to do he set himself a time limit. Walking home that evening, accordingly, he resolved that the book should be hunted out before he went to bed.

It was a mild evening. The sun had set; and in the long twilight the city seemed to him to be almost beautiful. For a moment he was tempted to linger, even to sit for a while on one of those stones by the wayside where beggar waifs perched by day, and watch the ebb and flow of color in the sky; then he thought of his home, his wife, the meal that would be waiting for him—he was hungrier than usual, the coffee had been well diluted—and he quickened his step.

After dinner, as he usually did, Dandekar wandered out into the open courtyard where his cane easy chair was kept. It was too big to go anywhere else, with its long leg rests that were an extension of the arms, and he had bought it only after they had acquired the ground-floor tenancy and had the courtyard in which to put it. The Bombay fornicator, Joseph said it was called, and after some initial outrage he found the idea pleased him. It was a vastly comfortable chair, and he knew once he sat in it the next stage was bed. With stern thoughts of his duty before him, however, he resisted the chair and sat instead on the mat that Sarojini had spread, and which she herself preferred to any chair. In a few minutes she joined him. Sensibly, she still used plantain leaves, so that they never had all that business of washing and scouring that their more progressive friends, who had taken to plates, did. She was, he reflected, a sensible woman in all the practical matters of life. There was a time when he had wanted plates too, but the idea had just been shelved and shelved and now he was glad; it was nicer to have a wife to talk to instead of one that sat by the tap, washing dishes.

"Had a nice day?" This was perfunctory; he was not really interested in Sarojini's day, and he was always grateful to her for keeping her account of it brief.

"Not bad." Sarojini handed him his *pan*, the neat cone of betel leaf with its subtle insertions of coconut and areca. "The children have been good and for once I managed to get some work out of Janaki . . . but really we must get another maid." She dismissed the subject. "And you?"

He settled himself as comfortably as he could, on this mat, and began an account of the day's doings. Actually there was seldom much doing; it was, in the main, gossip that he had to retail, but by exaggerating a foible here, substituting a better story ending there, he contrived to make it as interesting as he could. Over the years he had faithfully repeated most of the office conversations, except, naturally, those which dealt with sex—sex, that is to say, in its intimate aspects; he was as capable as the next man of discussing it in general terms. In fact he was talking about it now, relating Mahadevan's views on the nature of the beast in adolescent girls.

"So I told him," he continued, "it was only human nature for girls like our Ramabai to whisper and giggle when they see young men, there's nothing in it."

"Isn't there?"

"What?" He was astonished by the interruption, it happened so seldom.

"Anything more to it?"

"Yes, of course"—he moved uncomfortably—"but of course a well-brought-up girl from a respectable family isn't likely to—to—anyway there is not much opportunity, is there?" He was on surer ground here, and he felt better. "I mean you are in the house until she goes to school and when she comes back, and then on Sundays and holidays I am always at home."

"Yes, yes of course," she agreed.

He knew he ought to be satisfied, but somehow her

words chilled him. He did not take up the matter again but turned to other things, hoping to recapture peace, but as the evening progressed he found, unusually, that he had very little to say. He felt slightly cramped mentally and, he now realized, physically as well; then he recalled the reason for his self-imposed martyrdom and got up stiffly, gingerly placing his weight on each leg alternatively.

"I nearly forgot," he said, feeling more cheerful because he was about to do his duty. "Would you believe it, I specially sat on the mat to remind me, and until this moment I had clean forgotten. You had better give me the key, before I forget again."

"What key?"

"The key to the trunk. I must get rid of that book before one of the children gets hold of it."

"Oh, there's no danger of that," said Sarojini. "The trunk's locked, and I have the key."

"Well, it'll be one job done," urged Dandekar. "It won't take a minute, if you'll give me that key."

"I don't know where it is."

"Isn't it on the bunch?"

"It is usually. But it was getting so rusty I took it out the other day to oil it, and I don't know where I can have put it. I'll have a good search tomorrow and let you have it."

"All right." He sat down in his easy chair. "I must say I don't fancy rummaging in that old trunk this time of night. It'll be easier in the morning."

"Much easier." She smiled at him and rose, going in ahead of him to wash and prepare for bed as was their routine.

He sat on for some time after she had gone, thinking about the book and vaguely worrying about the missing key. There were other things in the trunk besides books: the silver cups presented to them at their wedding, one or two pieces of jewelry, and some of that gold tissue that his mother had given to the girls just before she died. Valuable things; and it was not as if they lived tight and secure in a house by themselves. There were eight families in this building, and the iron staircase connected all eight stories. Anyone could wander down at night and then, although they did keep the doors of their rooms closed, it would be a simple matter— At this stage he stood up, meaning to make a thorough search; but his wife and the children were asleep, and he found it an irksome business creeping around in the dark. Soon he gave up and went to bed.

# 4

HE slept badly. In the morning, a full two hours before it was time for them to rise, Chandru was up, screaming. "It's his teeth," said Sarojini with resigned acceptance, and she got out of bed to deal with the child, though with little success. Dandekar tossed and turned, trying vainly to sleep through the crying and crooning, and did in fact achieve a kind of dazed somnolence in which thieves appeared in alarming profusion, larger and more real than in life. He wrenched himself out of it at last, got up in case he should succumb again and sat on the edge of the bed, his head in his hands and staring at the floor. Then he saw that on the floor was his wife's bunch of keys with the silver chain that she tucked into her waistband—her skin had darkened there, through constant contact with the metal. He must have been staring at it for some time without perception; then eye and mind fused, and he bent and picked up the bunch. On it, a little to his surprise, he saw the trunk key. It had been cleaned and was brighter than the rest, otherwise he would hardly have noticed it. Sarojini must have found it last night after all, he thought, wondering why she hadn't told him. Maybe she thought he would start ransacking the box, despite the inappropriate hour. He smiled. Perhaps he would have done, at that. He knew what he was, once he had made up his mind to do something.

Next door the struggle was still going on. He was a good judge of these matters now, and he could tell by the sounds it would be another half hour before peace was restored. Half an hour by the clock—it was useless to time it any other way, one would just fret and imagine it was hours and hours. He glanced at the alarm clock, perilously poised on the narrow window ledge as many of their possessions were for want of a table. Half-past six. A long way yet to breakfast. He would do it now, he thought, while there was time on his hands, and he bent and dragged the trunk out from under the bed. It was heavy with the years' accumulations, and the books, he knew, were right at the bottom. He gave a little groan, heartfelt enough, yet sustained by the virtuous feeling of doing his duty; then he knelt down beside the box and opened it.

On top, in clean white mull and smelling of naphthalene, were Sarojini's two special-occasion saris, the lengths of gold tissue. Next the silver, wrapped like mummies, their identities lost in layers of linen bandage. He lifted these out. Underneath was a child's exercise book with stiff covers. He opened it, flicking the leaves and wondering which of his daughters' brilliant outpourings their mother wished to preserve, and as he did so a photograph fell out. He picked it up, staring at the face that gazed benignly back at him, his heart thumping loudly as his mind raced in mounting agitation. He did not know the man, he was sure of that. He was equally sure it was not one of his wife's relatives—after fifteen years of marriage he knew the lot. A friend then? He dismissed the thought. A married woman did not have men friends who were not known to the husband, the family. One of the girl's idols perhaps—a teacher, a film actor. Well, it might be, he said to himself, while his uncompromising mind withdrew into some forbidding fastness of its own, from where it emerged later, and again and again without cease, until at last he frantically repudiated the lie with which he had hoped to buy his peace.

In the next room his son's squalls were diminishing. He could see the girl Janaki (who had by now arrived, late as usual) whisking between courtyard tap and kitchen, and hear his wife's voice directing her. Which meant that whatever childish crisis it was was over, and the women could turn to the business of living. Dandekar listened intently for a few seconds longer, then he hurriedly repacked the trunk, locked it and thrust it back under the bed. He had just finished and was sitting on the bed, the keys still in his hand, when Sarojini came in. She looked a little tired in the morning light, there were purplish rings under her eyes that he had never noticed before, but she had washed and tidied herself, and her clothes and hair were clean and neat. He looked at her and quickly away, feeling oddly guilty as if she had discovered him in some prying meanness, then he forced himself to meet her gaze.

"Your keys," he croaked, and had to clear his throat before he could continue. "They were lying on the floor."

"I must have dropped them in my hurry this morning." She took the keys from him and tucked the chain securely into her waistband. "By the way," she said, "I found the trunk key last night. I meant to tell you, but I must have fallen asleep."

He should have said: "I know. I opened the trunk this morning." Then he should have asked, bluntly: "Whose photograph is it that I found in it, inside an exercise book?"

He could not. All the way to the office he asked himself why, and the farther he got from his home the more inexplicable became his conduct, until by the time he arrived he had persuaded himself that only the morning rush had prevented him from putting so simple a question. But when he got home, and the evening stretched before them leisurely, the question stuck in his throat. For the life of him he could not get it out. He sat in his easy chair, tense, watching his wife as she sat calm and cross-legged beside him, embroidering, wondering perhaps for the first time what went on in that smooth dark head and with some pale inkling at last that only the outermost fringes of conscious thought are ever communicated.

"What is wrong?"

He was startled. He had looked in the glass and his face, it seemed to him, betrayed nothing. What had Sarojini noticed?

"Nothing is wrong. Why do you ask?"

"You seemed very quiet."

He pondered. He had done his best, and had thought the flow of his conversation had not been noticeably impeded, but obviously he had deluded himself.

"I had rather a tiring day at the office," he said. "I didn't sleep too well last night either."

"Go to bed early," she said.

He got up. "Perhaps I will."

But when he was in bed he could not sleep. He twisted and turned, listening to the bed creaking under him, then he lay still as Sarojini came in and lay down but he could not hold it, restlessness was upon him like the plague. Sarojini had slept in that brief respite; then her breathing grew shallow and he could tell she was awake although she lay quite still. He threshed again, lost to all considera-

tion, and felt her hand on his forehead, softly stroking it.
In his misery he turned to her, throwing his arms across
her body and intending only to draw comfort from her
nearness, but at his touch he could feel her withdrawing—
gently enough but decisively. He kept his arm where it
was, lifeless and heavy from the rebuff, and felt her inert
and closed under him. He might have been a stranger—an
unwelcome one.

In the morning, shaving, he looked at himself closely,
moving around the room, looking glass in hand, to where
there was maximum light, scrutinizing forehead, mouth,
the skin around the eyes where the telltale lines might be,
certain at last that nothing showed. But when he got to
the office Kannan the peon, whom he met at the gate,
asked with sympathy if he didn't feel too well.

"Of course I'm well. Why for heaven's sake do you
think I'm not?"

The peon recoiled from this ill temper, then he rallied.

"I only asked. There's no harm in asking, is there? And
if you want to know, I don't think you can be well, biting
my head off like that."

Dandekar ground his teeth. The old fool! he said to himself, but he did not wish to argue and went silently inside.
The first person he met was Joseph, who was hanging up
his coat.

"My God," said Joseph. "What's the matter with you? You look as if your wife's run away and left you."

"Well, she hasn't," said Dandekar sourly, cursing Joseph and the slant of his mind. "She isn't likely to, either."

"I wouldn't be too sure. Women are sly cats, you never know what they're going to be up to next."

Ordinarily Dandekar would have said, pointedly, "Maybe your kind of women." But today he felt dispirited, vulnerable, in no way able to put up that robust defense which only the happily untested, or the blessedly unthinking, can; and somewhere around the perimeter of his mind, seeking entry, snuffled the thought: All women are the same.

The officers came in half an hour after the clerks, and from then until the coffee break the office was kept busy.

Dandekar, therefore, had something like two hours' peace, except for a few minutes when he went into Chari's room to take his instructions and Chari had looked up at him casually and pleasantly, then less casually, although he had said nothing. That look disturbed Dandekar; but he could not challenge his chief, could not say to him: "Look here, if you think there's something wrong with me say so, I'd just as soon know." But even as he formulated the thought Chari turned to the day's work, and minutes and memoranda buried his personal concerns.

At coffeetime they crowded in on him again, so that he

did not join in the general conversation, paying only as much attention as would save him from being conspicuous. It did not save him.

"An excellent arrangement," he heard Sastri say, then they were all looking at him, waiting for his contribution, and because Sastri was fairly sound and usually in accord with him, he thought it safe to echo approvingly, "An excellent arrangement."

There was a silence. Sastri looked at him in mild astonishment and, too late, Dandekar realized he had missed the overtones of sarcasm in his comment.

"Well, really," he said, "I should hardly have thought that you of all people, Dandekar— Anyhow, excellent or not, I really do not see how it could work."

"It worked in the picture." Joseph chuckled. "It was a very funny picture."

"I do not think a Box-and-Cox marriage is funny." Sastri sounded quite distressed. "I must say I do not, even in a film. I don't know what our government is coming to, allowing all this Western immorality to be shown in our country."

"But it was so funny," Joseph repeated, still laughing. "The husband—he was a night worker, you see—would go out then this other chap would slip in, then just as soon as he had gone to work in would come the husband. Everyone in the cinema just rolled with laughter." He

told them the whole story, thereby considerably diminishing the pleasure of two of his colleagues who subsequently went to see this same picture.

"All this could only happen in a film." Sastri dismissed
the story. "Do you really think any husband wouldn't
suspect something was going on?"

"Why should he, if his wife was clever as this woman
was?"

"Servants talk," said Sastri. "If there was anything like
it going on, be sure there would be endless gossip."

"Which the husband would be the last one to hear,"
said Joseph.

"But if he asked them?"

"Why should he, if he suspected nothing?"

"Supposing he went home early one day before the man
had left?"

"I don't know." Joseph was getting a little irritated.
Really, Sastri was much too literal; how could one ever
enjoy a film or a detective story if one picked such earnest
holes in them? "I suppose if he did the fat would be in the
fire. But it didn't," he said pointedly, "happen in the film
I've just told you about."

"Films are not life." Sastri looked around, quietly tri-
umphant. "That is the case I wished to establish."

So far it had been a duologue. Dandekar had held his
tongue though there were several points he would have

liked to contest—had held quiet in the hope that his slip would be forgotten, but it was not to be. Sastri turned to him.

"As for you, Dandekar, I'm really surprised to find you take such a frivolous view of marriage—you, a married man—"

"I didn't—" began Dandekar.

"—with a respectable wife and two young daughters—"

"I didn't mean what I said at all," said Dandekar. "I—"

"Then why say it?"

"I wasn't thinking."

"That's when the truth comes out," cried Joseph, "when the guards are asleep! Sly dog, Dandekar!"

Dandekar could have hit Joseph. Instead in silent fury he consigned him and his humor to everlasting rebirth, and suppressed any retort.

Then it was time to go back to their desks.

# 5

DANDEKAR walked slowly, going home that night. Usually his step was brisk, because although he was invariably tired by the end of the day there was the thought of a well-cooked meal, his wife's welcome, the children, his home, to spur him on. But tonight his thoughts were somber, linked to pain deep in his bowels or his breast— which, he could hardly say—because the certainties on which he had rested so long seemed to be sliding—not so much that he toppled, but enough to suggest to him that he had not built on rock. On what then had he built? On the sands which wise men said all mortal men's hopes were based? Desert sands that sang as they shifted, driving a man mad before they engulfed him? He had heard the story in boyhood from a Musulman, a crazy old man who roamed the bazaar, delighting children with tales of the Gobi desert in which he claimed to have wandered. Dandekar shivered. He could almost hear that eerie song, feel the sand beneath his feet. With an effort he rid himself of sound and sense, and found they were succeeded by emptiness, as if he were walking in a void.

It was new to him, this feeling. Bewildered, he tried to grasp it, place it, kill it. It was beyond him.

"I have been starving a whole week, seven days and nights."

The voice reached him, disembodied, and he thought, That's it, that's how I feel; then he heard the begging wine, the slap of the concave belly, and he recollected himself.

"A coin, I beseech you." The beggar again. "I am starving."

"Are you?" Dandekar's voice was gentle.

"I have not eaten for a week." It was his mechanical plea, but behind it the beggar's eyes were wary. One had to be careful, when a man was in this mood; he either gave a lot or nothing.

"Do you know how it feels?" He tapped his stomach. "Not hungry. Just empty, sick and empty."

Dandekar hesitated, then he turned away. There were beggars everywhere; between office and home, daily, he saw at least a score. He walked on.

"Miser and son of a miser!" The beggar's voice was harsh with disappointment. "You will remember this, one day. You will be sorry—"

Dandekar walked faster. He did not want to hear, today, these curses and threats. They meant nothing, they were powerless; but he did not want to hear.

But at the next suppliant voice he gave in. Usually well provided with small change, today all he could find was a rupee. He drew it from his pocket, uncaring, and flung it to the beggar, watching while the man retrieved it from the dust and turned to look at him with eyes that knew that here was a brain in ferment while the practiced mouth poured forth its mechanical blessings. Then Dandekar moved on quickly, determined to hear no more begging voices, and after a time, very soon, his engrossed mind took charge, shutting out all extraneous sound without conscious effort on his part.

Why had Sarojini lied? Had she? Was she playing some matrimonial game? Was it conceivable, feasible, that she might? "No," he said stoutly. It was all that poppycock office talk that had done the damage. But he had begun to be troubled before all that poppycock talk, otherwise it would have flowed harmlessly over him leaving him careless and buoyant instead of half-drowned as now. He shivered. His imagination had developed unwonted power, it was an almost physical sensation. "Of course I'm not half-drowned, I'm nowhere near water," he said aloud, but he had no sooner hauled himself out of this swamp than he could feel his lively mind preparing to thrust him into another. "I'll not think about it until I reach home," he said again aloud, louder than was prudent, and this time did not escape turning heads, startled faces. He closed his lips tightly, and until he reached home conscientiously listened to every beggar's and hawker's plea.

When he got home Sarojini was not there. His oldest daughter, Ramabai, was in charge of the sleeping baby, and she met him with a look of importance on her face and her finger to her lips.

"Where is your mother?" he whispered, duly cautioned.

"Back soon," breathed Ramabai, full of responsibility, and tiptoed back to the child's room.

Again that uncomfortable sense of strangeness in his own home descended on Dandekar. He did not know what to do with himself. He stood irresolute, wondering where Sarojini could have got to this time and if it was as before; then he thought he would ask the maid. She might know. She might also know about that previous occasion. "Servants gossip," came the echoes of office poppycock talk, making him feel awkward and guilty. But who on earth would gossip with that imbecile? he said to himself angrily. All I'm going to do is to put a straightforward question and ask for a rational answer. But he did not feel any easier as he prowled in search of her and when he could not find her he lost his head.

"Janaki," he thundered, "Janaki!"

A number of things, it seemed to him, happened at once. He had not heard Sarojini's light step, and she appeared to take shape beside him out of the thickening evening gloom. Ramabai shot out of the child's room, her face shocked and reproving. And Chandru began to cry.

He was alone. They were comforting the child, as of course they must. Dandekar sat down in the courtyard to wait. He was in the wrong, he knew, but the feeling of guilt only added to his grievance. After all, what had he done, apart from summoning his maid in perhaps too loud tones? It was an innocent action, and innocence was surely enough to protect one against one's chiding self. Or was it? He felt it ought to be, but he did not know. He stared at the tulasi tree, wondering. Its glossy green leaves were almost black in the gloom, but the polished brass of its stand caught and reflected every stray gleam of light. It was particularly bright tonight, he noticed, as if Sarojini had freshly burnished it. But why today? he wondered. Sarojini polished it on puja day, which was either Thursday or Friday, he never could remember which, and today was—what was it? Tuesday, he decided, dredging his sluggish mind for the information. What was his wife up to, polishing the tulasi stand on a Tuesday? He shook himself. Did it really matter which day she chose to polish brass? But the irritating grit remained.

He was still brooding on this when Sarojini came out. She looked quite calm and serene, and for a fleeting instant he wondered whether women's nerves were tougher, that they could stand such fiendish noise without perceptible signs of wear, then he remembered what had caused the uproar.

"Janaki," he said abruptly. "What has happened to that miserable good-for-nothing?"

"She's gone," said Sarojini. "I sent her packing."

"Dismissed her?" He stared at her suspiciously. "Why?"

"She was good for nothing," said Sarojini. "You just said so yourself."

He was nonplused, then his thoughts grew darker. She had done it to foil him; being clever she had guessed what lay in his mind and forestalled him.

"Why didn't you tell me?"

"Why should I?" Her eyes were puzzled. "Really, what is the matter with you? You've never before concerned yourself with the servants."

He was put on the defensive, and retreated. "No . . . I just don't want you to have to do everything yourself."

"Don't worry," said Sarojini. "I've engaged another girl. I settled the matter this evening, actually, otherwise I'd have been in earlier."

Her manner was calm, her face serene. No woman touched with guilt ever looked like this. He believed this, and he tried to relax. But somewhere nibbled the thought: What if the issues are big enough? Big enough to call for the supreme effort of glazing over passion and emotion with this innocent quiet?

The rest of the evening he spent passing between violent trust and extreme mistrust. It gave an uneven edge to the conversation, their relationship, which tired not only him but, he could see, also Sarojini. Nevertheless, doggedly, he stayed up until the usual hour, intending while he hung on somehow to question her tactfully about the photograph. It had to be tactful. The blunt question was beyond him; it stuck in his throat, and he had by now acknowledged that he could not get it out. It might hurt her, he tried to fool himself, but he knew it was a lack of courage. The evening wore on, while he hunted around for tactful ways of leading to the subject. In desperation he determined to try the mechanical expedient by which he often gained results; he would set himself a time, say an hour from now, before the passing of which he would question her.

There was still a few minutes' grace when Sarojini said quietly, "What is the matter with you?"

"Nothing. Why do you ask?"

"You've been looking at your watch as if you were afraid of missing a train."

"At this time of night?" He laughed hoarsely. "No, of course not. It must be a bad habit starting."

He looked again at his watch, brushing a hand over his eyes so that she could not see. About ten seconds to go. He cleared his throat and said, inanely, "We were talking about photographs in the office this morning."

"Oh, were you?"

He could see she was stifling a yawn. He felt a little sorry for her, briefly, but his affairs were more pressing.

"Yes. We were saying how extraordinary it was how people keep photographs, even if it's someone they hardly know."

"Yes, isn't it? I was only saying to myself the other day—"

He was astounded. He had actually succeeded in arousing her interest with his preposterous remarks.

"—saying that really at my age it's time to stop being sentimental. Do you know the other day I came across a photo of one of my old music teachers? I can only just remember him now, though at the time—"

"Do you mean the one in the trunk?" He could not help the urgency in his voice, and he seemed to surprise her.

"Why, yes, I believe that's where it is—how did you know? Now he was—"

A vast, overpowering sense of relief came over him. The leaden weight that had been dragging him down, bodily, spiritually, lifted. He felt lightheaded. He loved his wife, he was grateful to her, he was a fool and worse to have doubted her. In the sudden upsurge of love he wanted at once to possess her and to lay his head in her lap and be comforted. Instead, awkwardly, he took her hand in both his own and fondled it. This was as far as he could let himself go, after fifteen years of marriage, in this quadrangle open to the sky and the seven other families above.

Desire grew, when as was her practice she went in before him to wash and get ready for bed. He fidgeted while he waited for her, wondering impatiently why she should be as it seemed to him longer than ever tonight. Then she was done. He washed hurriedly, changed and got into bed beside her, his heart thumping wildly even now, the prelude. For a few seconds he lay still, then he laid his hand between her breasts and rested it there, feeling the quiet heartbeats, the smooth skin, her warmth. It was the signal, unvoiced, mutually understood, that he would take her now, soon, while his caressing hand moved from tenderness to passion, sometimes slowly and sometimes almost without pause. Tonight he was burning, could hardly contain himself. But when she felt his urgent movement she took his hand and laid it down by her side. "Not tonight," she said gently, and turned away.

He subsided, and lay limp and quiet beside her, thinking. She never refused him unless she had some reason, and turning it over in his mind he could think of none. He might have been mortified, but was too bewildered. After all these years was he to suffer as certain of his colleagues did? Belligerence flared, slightly, and he thought of asserting himself over her. But he was not sure he could rekindle his passion, and moreover there was a delicacy in his nature, almost unsuspected, which precluded it.

But it wasn't an old photograph of an old music teacher. He woke up with the thought. Somewhere, efficiently, his meticulous brain had filed away an exact description and now blindly, impervious to his peace of mind, produced it for inspection. So far from being an old one it was very new. He remembered it absolutely clearly: the vivid black and white of the print, the natural pose of the subject—even the high gloss was unmarked. Pictures like that weren't taken twenty years ago. Nevertheless he felt he ought to check, look at it again to make sure, more from a desperate masochism than any real doubts that he had, but there was not time. He was late as it was, and he hadn't the patience or time to dodge about waiting for the coast to be clear before getting hold of his wife's keys and opening the trunk. All the same he wasted a quarter of an hour trying, earning for himself curious looks from the new hireling. He castigated the girl silently, briefly, before hurrying to the bus stop.

There was a time—why, less than a week ago, he said to himself queerly—when his life had stretched before him even and serene, and he could say with assurance that at this time in the morning he would be in the office, that at such a time he would wake with Sarojini by his side. It was an assurance that comforted him—a certainty of living which he craved and which he had never coveted until now that he had touched the extreme fringe of its ephemerality.

And last week, if the hypothetical case had been put to him, he would have known exactly what to do. The husband must demand the keys from his wife, making no pretext but saying plainly what it was he was after; thereafter open the trunk and inspect the photograph; and thereafter if he did not deem it to be as his wife said— At this point he stopped. He did not know what came next. Or did he know and not care to admit it?

"Dandekar! Really, what has come over the man?"

"Nothing has come over me. Why?"

"He asks why! This is the second time he has picked up my cup and—"

Dandekar put down the cup. He found Joseph's facetious manner of speaking as if he weren't there acutely annoying, but he was at fault and he apologized, grumbling a little under his breath.

"When a man does that," pursued Joseph, "there's something on his mind. Otherwise—"

"Oh leave him alone," said Sastri good-naturedly. "He's probably had a rotten night— Was it that brat of yours again, Dandekar?"

Dandekar wanted to say, boldly and truthfully, "I was

thinking about the difference between theory and practice," then he hesitated. They might take him up, ask specifically what theory, which practice, and he was not sure, with the pestilential Joseph there, that he could carry it off. A bad night was a good let out, and prudently he took it.

But later—soon afterwards, in fact—he began to wonder why Sastri had considered it necessary to provide him with a ready excuse. Did Sastri *know* he had something on his mind, and if so how? He stared suspiciously at his friend, and not for the first time—though he had only recently taken to doing so—wondered what thoughts and deeds and the births of deed were locked in a man's skull, beneath the bones and the scalp and the fair façade.

Sastri intercepted the glance. It startled him. When they were packing up that evening, out of earshot of the others, he said kindly, "Spend the night with us, Dandekar. A good night's sleep can work wonders. I'm sure Sarojini won't mind."

Dandekar jumped as if stung. "No. No thank you," he said stiffly.

But Sastri was of the stuff that friends are made of. He said so to himself, frequently: "That's what friends are for—to help." For several evenings following he walked part of the way home with Dandekar, chatting amiably if forcedly of this and that. Dandekar, even in his misery, was touched. It meant a very long walk for Sastri, whose house lay in the opposite direction, and he knew Sastri was as fond of his creature comforts as any.

"Kind of you to accompany me," he said awkwardly. "I—"

"Nonsense, my dear fellow. Enjoy it."

Dandekar smiled bleakly. "Hardly, these days. Truth is I haven't—haven't been feeling myself lately."

"We all have bad patches."

"Fact is, I'm a little worried about things at home."

"The children?"

"No. They're fine."

"Sarojini?"

"No!"

Sastri knew now what it was. Dandekar saw the knowledge in his eyes and cursed himself for the overloud voice, the too emphatic denial. He tried to retrieve the blunder.

"In a way it is Sarojini. She—she doesn't seem able to run the house as well as she used to. I suppose women have their—their bad patches, same as we do, as you said."

"Yes, yes, of course."

"It'll pass, of course—it's just a matter of a week or two."

"Of course. These little—upsets—seldom last much longer."

"One must be patient."

"Yes."

They were talking meaninglessly, exchanging words like coins which both knew to be counterfeit, while their minds quietly fused, acknowledging one to the other that both knew something was very wrong with Sarojini.

# 6

THE month wore on, the bus fares accumulated, though Dandekar hardly thought about them. He walked because it had become a habit, not to save money any more, and when at the end of the month he realized he *had* saved money he did not know what to do with it. Buy something for the children? His heart was not in it. For Sarojini? Nor for her, he thought bleakly. Soaps and scents and sweet-smelling oils were for the woman you loved and possessed, not for— He pulled himself up short. Did he not love Sarojini? Had he not possessed her? Of course, he said to himself resolutely, in misery, remembering only the nights that she wordlessly withdrew herself from him. Normally he seldom went to her more than once a week; now in his uncertain frenzy he tried night after night, unable to accept her refusal, unable to keep from her, equally unable to enforce his demands.

He should, he told himself, have asked bluntly why

she refused him. With an effort, one night, he had asked her what was wrong. Nothing, she had whispered, and he had let it go. That was a mistake. He should have insisted. But brutal insistences like these, as much as physical ones, were beyond his nature.

Or was he afraid she might tell him his body repulsed her? That there was some other man? The insidious thought crept in and took hold. He tried to shake it off angrily. He was quite capable of facing the truth. The truth, whatever it was, was better than this uncertainty. In theory. In any case Hindu wives were not like that; they married for life, did not look at another man. Yet times were changing. "But not so fast," he cried furiously, "nor so far as to touch the older generation like me, like my wife. We are stable." When he had said that he cowered a little. "Stable, God willing," he amended, walking quickly on.

"Master, a coin I beg of you. One from the many with which God has blessed you."

Dandekar swore under his breath and stopped. He realized he had been jingling the coins in his pocket like an invitation to every loafer within earshot to batten on him.

"I work for my money," he said sourly. "Every anna has been earned."

"With God's help," said the beggar. "God helps those who help themselves."

"But not to other people's money," said Dandekar, temporarily lifted out of his depression.

"No, sir, no. But blessed is he who gives."

"Happy is he who receives, also."

"True, master." The beggar smiled disarmingly. "Yet happiness spreads, such is its quality; the giver is also bene-fited."

"Your technique is excellent," said Dandekar without rancor, and he took out a coin. It was a rupee. He shrugged; what did it matter? He hadn't known what to do with the money anyway; and maybe the benefits would be correspondingly larger. He began to smile at that, working out the contribution to have his peace re-stored, but he had not walked far before depression closed in on him again. It had been a brief respite, despite the rupee.

He reached home early. His daughters were not wait-ing on the threshold to receive him and his gifts and he was not surprised. They would not be expecting him at this time, nor would Sarojini. He grew still. Sarojini. He ought to call out to her as he usually did in case she thought him an intruder, walk boldly in because she knew his step. He did not. He bent down and removed his sandals, then softly in bare feet he walked into his house.

Inside he had to pause for a moment or two while his eyes grew accustomed to the gloom—light fell sparsely in this courtyard, hemmed in by long gray walls. Then he saw Sarojini sitting cross-legged on the uneven cement floor in front of the tulasi tree. She had her back to him, and there was a curious rigidity in her worship that made him uneasy. What did she lack, or suffer, to pray so intensely? He moved toward her irresolutely, a step or two, unwilling to intrude yet impelled on. Then he stopped. Four votive lamps were alight, one at each corner of the tulasi's brass as customary; but a fifth had been lit and burned steadily in front of a portrait of the man Sarojini had said was her music teacher. It was the same man. The single wick threw a pale glow on features which were embedded in his mind, gleamed on the tinseled jasmine garland hung about the picture. Dandekar felt himself shiver. This was a man, and his wife had garlanded him as if he were a god.

The light breeze of evening was stirring. The demure flames in the silver lampions began dancing in wild shapes. Dandekar, roused at last, turned softly and went out as quietly as he had come in.

Outside he stood stockstill, a little dazzled by the light after the gloom of the courtyard, bewildered and uncomprehending of what he had seen, and finding extraordinary the ordinary, familiar sights of the street scene. Jerkily he began to walk, with no notion of where he was going, and wanting only to get as far away from his home as he could. For the first mile or two he was too numb to think. Vivid images, tableaux of what he had seen, imagined, dreamed, flashed through his mind and he let them go; they were drawings without captions. But presently he began to supply them—hesitantly, because here was something he did not understand, and it frightened him a little. Sarojini had lied to him. Either through love, or through fear, and he could think of no other reason, she reverenced a man unknown to him, her husband. She kept a photograph of him in a locked trunk. She had set up a portrait of him and bedecked it as if it were some kind of god. Was this man, then, some kind of god to her? Physically? Spiritually? He began to sweat, floundering in depths which he felt were beyond him. Beyond him, and unfair to him. What had he done, to be tangled in a mystery which threatened to disrupt the whole of his life? Indignation rose, temporarily ousting fear. He did not deserve it. He would find out all about what was going on and put an end to it. How exactly, he did not know. It would mean watching his wife, he supposed, changing his routine to catch her unawares. What else? He did not know, but glimpsed vaguely a long and sorry vista of deliberate interruptions to the ordered harmony of his life.

He began, now, to walk homewards again, trying to think intelligently of ways and means. He would stay at home tomorrow and watch his wife's movements—that was a good first step. No, not tomorrow; he would have to ask for a day's leave first. Day after tomorrow then. He would set out as usual for the office and—

"Cousin! Cousin Dandekar!"

He stopped. It was his wife's Cousin Rajam calling to him from the opposite side of the street. He knew it was useless to walk on, to pretend he hadn't heard; she would run after him, shouting, sublimely free of all self-consciousness. She had started to cross the street already, undeterred by a string of bullock carts. Life goes on, he thought morosely; whatever the crises into which one was plunged one had to come up, put aside one's sweated and anguished thinking to deal with these irrelevancies.

"Cousin, what are you doing here?"

The last bullock passed, speeded on its way by a sharp slap on its rump from the impatient Rajam. She was across, hurling questions at him as if it were her right.

"I'm not doing anything," he said shortly. "Just going for a walk."

"Where to?"

"Nowhere special."

"It's quite late."

"I know." Irritated, he thought it would check her if he asked some of the questions, although he suspected she would be only too willing to answer. She has nothing to hide either, he thought hopelessly, no reason not to tell me why she is here. The innocent are free. "It's late for you to be out too," he said nevertheless. "What has kept you?"

"Well." She lowered her voice. "I've just been to the market . . . you know how it is, if you wait until everyone has gone everything is much cheaper, sometimes you even get something for nothing . . . one has to eke out one's pension, Cousin Dandekar."

He felt sorry for her, perhaps for the first time since they had become cousins by marriage. My misfortune has softened me, he thought. Perhaps this is what our priests mean, when they say suffering purifies. On an impulse he took out a rupee and pressed it into her palm.

"It must be difficult to manage," he said awkwardly, closing her fingers over the coin.

"Really, Cousin! How kind you are!" Surprised and pleased—twice as overcome as anyone else would have been—she heaped blessings on him. He managed to mutter a farewell in the middle of the gush and hurried on, but a last stray blessing caught his attention:

". . . and may God grant health to Sarojini."

He turned. "Is Sarojini ill?"

"Why, no, Cousin." His sharp voice had startled Rajam. "But is it not usual to wish one's relatives health and happiness?"

"Not always." He knew it was folly, but he said it. She glowered at him, her mouth pursed and plainly rebuking, but she still held his money in her hand.

"You are not yourself, Cousin," she contented herself with saying.

"Not myself," Dandekar repeated, walking furiously on. Well, he was not himself because his wife was not herself, because in marriage you acted and reacted one upon the other, however much you wished it otherwise, and whether you wanted to or no.

It was after ten when he reached home. From the street he could see the lanterns of night watchmen, making their rounds of the larger houses, occasionally hear their lonely cry—call and answer, answer, answer, like an echoing cave from each watchman who heard.

He walked in softly, in case Sarojini was asleep, but she was waiting for him, quietly embroidering in her accustomed place.

"You're late."

It was not an indictment, not even a question. She simply made a statement of fact. She had never done otherwise, he thought fleetingly, she had been a good wife. Was and is, he amended, and amended that still further to: Was and will be.

"The children wanted to wait up," she continued, "but I said no, not in term time. I don't think it does them any good, these late nights."

Her voice was even, if anything she asked for an endorsement of her action. Nevertheless he felt guilty; she would have been fully justified in accusing him of letting the children down, and her forbearance made him uncomfortable.

"We were working late," he said lamely, following her into the kitchen. "I hadn't time to get them anything."

"I guessed that. Of course I had no way of telling how late you would be."

No, he thought, only officers can afford luxuries like telephones, and a call to make sure the servants bring up your meal piping hot. Still, Sarojini always had a hot meal for him, even if he had to wait for it. There had been one occasion, he remembered, when he had come home at midnight—this was during British days, on the eve of a viceregal visit when everything had to be whitewashed, more spick and span than ever a normal working office could be—and even at this late hour Sarojini had produced a sizzling-hot meal. Her voice brought him back to the present.

"It's just curds and rice," she was saying, uncovering the dish before him. "I didn't know when you'd be in, I thought it would be best to have something cold."

He ate silently, not knowing what he was eating. In all the years of their marriage this had not happened to him, and although he told himself it was a small matter, too childish for a grown man to worry over, yet his heart was tight to bursting.

# 7

CHARI, the head of the department, was away on short leave. That was the first thing that registered when Dandekar got to the office the next day. Chari actually had gone on leave three days ago, and only the turmoil of the previous evening had made him forget this fact. Now, without pleasure, Dandekar faced the prospect of asking Ghose, Chari's deputy, for the day off that he desperately needed. Ghose was almost a foreigner—a man from the North who spoke differently and thought differently from the clerks, most of whom were Southerners. Dandekar did not dislike foreigners—after all he had, and not so long ago, worked under an Englishman and harmoniously at that. Yet he would very much rather have faced Chari with his request than Ghose, and only the urgency of his affairs drove him to the latter.

Ghose was young, keen, an M.A. of Calcutta University with a Cambridge degree squashed on top of that to make sure the world would not overlook him. He had a burning, painful pride in the new India, coupled with an acute sensitivity to its shortcomings which made him rather more earnest than he might have been. That morning, with Chari away, he was particularly harassed. Chari had learned—from his English captors, a curious legacy of his jailbird past—to be casual, and his casualness was apt to conceal, as Ghose was discovering, the solid slabs of work he could get through in a day. When therefore Dandekar, dry-mouthed and hesitant, asked for a day's leave he said sharply, instead of nodding in the absent-minded way Chari had, "Leave? Why?"

Dandekar was taken aback. In all his years of service he had never asked leave for frivolous reasons. He had assumed in turn that his requests would never be questioned. The little composure he had managed to summon withered away now, like severed vines left lying in the sun, and he said, stammering:

"For—for personal reasons."

"What personal reasons?"

Dandekar's heart began to hammer. What could he give as a reason—that he wanted to shadow his wife? He recoiled from the thought. He had lost the assurance to improvise. Yet he must say something—he could not stand in front of this desk like a mute forever. Dimly into

71

his mind, now, came echoes of conversations in the outer office—the glib answers of practiced people to pointed questions.

"My aunt has died," he said. "I must attend to the funeral rites."

Ghose fumed. It had become an international joke, the number of aunts and cousins Indians had whose funerals it was imperative for them to attend. Well, the international jokers must go elsewhere for their laughs. He said stiffly:

"When did she die?"

Dandekar was speechless. Why the questioning? He could not go on lying, and he could not give his reason. But his need for leave was genuine, urgent, real—was that not enough for this man?

Ghose's doubts had crystallized with Dandekar's silence.

"I'm afraid I cannot sanction your leave," he said formally, then his eyes met the stricken clerk's, and certitude and composure deserted him.

"I'm sorry," he said, stammering in his turn, "but we are—are exceptionally busy just now . . . any other time I would have had no—no hesitation—"

Dandekar's face changed color. He still did not say anything but simply turned and went out.

Dandekar's two worlds were his office and his home, and he had been fortunate so far in that one could usually balance the other. His worries over children's illnesses, the intractability of servants, relatives' insufferableness, he usually forgot in office routine, or they were diminished in the greater woes of his colleagues. Or if he had suffered harshness or injustice in the office, Sarojini's indignation, the extra comfort with which she took care to surround him, soon put things in their proper perspective.

Now, going home, they loomed large. The clash with Ghose had angered him, and when the anger was gone it left something worse, a leaden depression which he could not shake off. He would have given anything to have told Sarojini, to have had her ready sympathy which he knew would instantly have lifted his spirit out of this morass. He could not. He had his meal, he asked after the children, and he watched her. Was she, too, walking in some wasteland, wandering hopelessly? Unable to cry except silently? Lost and alone? No. She was not alone. His blood began to pound again at the thought; he turned his face so that she might not see, waited until the storm had subsided, then said brusquely he was going to bed.

Dandekar did not go to the office the following day. The need to do something overwhelmed and possessed him. Whatever the consequences, he must find out what his wife was up to, put his house in order.

In the morning, craftily, he carried out his habitual routine—not automatically as on ordinary days, but con-

sciously referring back to what he had done yesterday—
all the yesterdays of his past real life, not this last month
of nightmare. At precisely the same time he said good-by
to his wife. At precisely the same time he reached the
halfway milestone. There he stopped. He did not know
what to do next. Go back, keep watch on his wife and his
house? The neighbors might see, and what could he possibly say? Get someone to spy for him? Who? To whom
could he entrust this shameful act? He sweated, seized by
a kind of anxious terror. For a few seconds he looked
longingly at the milestone; it was equidistant between
office and home, and it would be as easy to go on as
go back. Easier, he thought with fright, and he turned
abruptly before the temptation could overcome him and
slowly walked back.

Their tenement house was one of a block of graying,
jerry-built structures that towered over the smaller, older
houses in the narrow street. As the tenements had grown,
eating up space, so the lanes that ran between the blocks
contracted, until now they existed as the narrowest of
alleys, barely allowing the ingress and egress of the tenants. It was in one of these that Dandekar decided to wait.
From here he could watch the street; and he had to trust
to luck, and to the semigloom of the alley, that nobody
he knew would see him.

He wondered, while he waited in the shadows, his
head furtively lowered, what he would do if Sarojini

came out. Follow her? She might only be going to market. Or what would he say if someone saw him? If Sarojini saw him? Or—

He almost fell then, as something hit him violently in the chest. Recovering himself he realized it was a sack of rice slumped over a laborer's shoulder and half obscuring his vision.

"Clumsy oaf!" he cried. "Why don't you look where you're going?"

"How can I, under this load? If it comes to that, could you not see me coming and make way?"

Dandekar breathed heavily. Really, the impudence of the working classes nowadays was beyond all bounds. But he did not want to quarrel, and he flattened himself silently against the wall. When the man had passed he returned to watching his house, wondering uneasily if Sarojini had slipped out in the meanwhile, and was brought out of his absorption by a tap on the shoulder. It was the laborer, returning with the empty sack.

Five sacks passed. At the sixth the man stopped, exasperated. "Really, master, is there nowhere else where you can spend your day?"

Dandekar slunk out. He could not afford to argue; a crowd would certainly collect. He walked to the next alley, but half a dozen street urchins were playing in it; he could not stand there like a ninepin among them. There was one other alley, but a family they knew lived in the overhanging block, and after some thought he decided the risk was too great. Now he did not know what to do. He could not walk on, he would have to pass his house. He could not turn back, and he did not relish loitering in the street. Then he thought of the small coffee shop not a hundred yards from the tenement. It was a cheap, noisy place, frequented by street louts and none too respectable—certainly no one of his class would go there; but it would be ideal for his purpose. Looking around to make sure he was unobserved by anyone who mattered, he went in, feeling unpleasantly conspicuous, and sat down at one of the iron tables. The view from here was excellent, much better than the alley. He couldn't miss her if she went out—always assuming she hadn't already gone.

The waiter brought his coffee. It was his third cup, and he had run out of small change. While he fumbled around in his pockets he became conscious that they were watching him. My God, he thought furiously, one can do nothing, nothing at all, without the whole world wanting to poke its nose in. He would have liked to punch one of those goggling faces, but they were street loafers only too ready for a fight, and he was a—a middle-aged clerk, he said to himself. I don't stand a chance in this company, I ought not to be in it—what am I doing here? He began to feel confused now and got up, half-blind, and blundered out. But he had not paid for his coffee. The waiter was after him, two waiters. He wanted to run, indeed he ran a step or two, then he took a grip on himself and turned savagely.

"Here is a rupee for your execrable coffee," he said to his gaping pursuer. "Keep the change."

He strode rapidly on, up the street, past his house; well, it did not matter now. Sarojini had had ample time to make her getaway. But at long last—perhaps through sheer pity—luck was with him. At first he would not recognize it. Red-and-green saris were common; Sarojini wasn't the only one who wore those colors. Nevertheless he quickened his pace, and as he came closer saw that it was Sarojini. She was walking quickly, her sari drawn over her head against the sun, and she walked without once turning her head. Well of course, he thought, she would have no notion that she was being followed. It made his task a little easier, but it was still by no means an easy one. There were the usual crowds in the streets, a great deal of distracting noise, scores of women in red and green. He found he had to concentrate to keep Sarojini in view, and it tired him, that and the glare—he could feel the pain building up behind his eyes. He kept doggedly on. He would find out where Sarojini was going or die in the attempt. Do it or die. Die or— He stopped. He could not see Sarojini. He had lost sight of her behind a group of shoppers—temporarily, he thought; but now she had vanished. He walked faster, forgetting his pain, ruthlessly pushing his way through the crowds and careless of the dark looks it earned him.

He gave up at last. Even while he tried he had known it was useless; there were a hundred lanes and alleys into which she might have turned. He began to make for home, having nothing else to do, remembered he was supposed to be at the office, and stopped uncertainly. He was tired out, emotionally as well as physically, and the two together imposed an intolerable strain on him. He looked around for somewhere to sit—he could stand no longer. Nearby in semishade he spotted a culvert lined with boulders, and on one of these he sank down thankfully.

He had yielded almost without thought to the need for rest; but as rest revived him he began to think again. In all probability Sarojini would come back the way she had gone, and if she did she could hardly miss seeing him. That was the last thing he wanted to happen, yet at the same time he did not want to move from where he was; there was a chance, just the bare chance, that she would not come back alone, and the desire to find out with whom she was consorting was consuming him like a fire. He got up, although he had no plan formulated. It was a blazing-hot day, and the street was full of bobbing black umbrellas warding off the sun. One of those would do, he thought, and a little to his own surprise found himself standing outside an umbrella shop. He went in, asked for one, paid what was asked. One part of him shrank back, appalled. He was a clerk, not a millionaire; ten rupees was one-twelfth of his monthly salary. But it was only a minute part of him that reacted normally, the rest did not care. He went back to the culvert, sat down with the spread umbrella.

It was late afternoon when she returned. She was not alone. Calmly he watched them come up the street, lowered his umbrella to conceal him as they drew level, folded it slowly when they had gone. Then he sat and waited, still quite calmly, until it was time to go home.

His chattering daughters were in. He exchanged banter with them, marveling that he sounded so natural. Chandru woke, wanting company; he held his son absently while Sarojini rearranged his cradle. The maidservant had some problem or other and he resolved it for her. All the time it was someone else—a stranger.

It was when the girls were asleep and the house was quiet, he and Sarojini sitting in their accustomed places in the courtyard, that he became aware of a change. The numbness was going. He began to feel like himself, instead of some performer in a dream. Covertly, now, he studied his wife. She looked the same to him, no different for all her philandering—a beautiful woman, despite the shadows under her eyes from sleepless nights with Chandru. A slow anger welled up inside him. He said, roughly, "You look well today."

"Do I?"

"Yes."

She smiled slightly. "You sound as if you wished I weren't."

He was silent. He could feel his rage working up inside him, but he did not want to give it vent—not yet. He said abruptly, "Enjoyed your outing today?"

"Outing? I haven't been anywhere special."

"Haven't you been out?"

"Oh yes . . . I go out every day, there's always something we need."

He wanted to torment her more, see her squirm on that hotbed of lies. "What did we need today?"

"Oh . . . er . . ." For the first time she seemed a little flustered. "Vegetables—fruit. Why?"

"What sort of fruit?"

"Any sort, it didn't matter . . . there was none in the house."

"What sort of fruit?"

"Mangoes."

He leaned forward to be cruel. "Mangoes," he repeated. "I would like one. I am very partial to fruit out of season."

She made to rise, but he caught her by the wrist and

pulled her down, and in that act of force he lost self-control.

"Mangoes," he cried, shaking her furiously. "So that's what you went out for. Not for anything else. No. Oh no. Just for a little fruit like a dutiful housewife. Like a loving wife. Like a thrifty whore—a—"

"For God's sake." Her face was colorless, sick.

"Which god? The god of love?"

"The children," she whispered. "You'll frighten them."

"Yes, the children." He stopped shouting and his voice was more deadly, killing in cold blood. "Did you stop to think of them before starting your shameless affair?"

"What affair?" She took her hands away from her face. He had never before seen it like this, naked and wet; she always covered her face when she wept.

"Your love affair with your music teacher."

She was staring at him; she had forgotten her lie. He said harshly, "It doesn't do to lie so easily, does it? It's like lighting a fire under your own—"

"Love affair," she burst out. "Love affair?"

"Yes. I saw you with your lover today." Suddenly all other feelings were swamped in anguish. He was sobbing as nakedly as she had been. "I never thought such a thing was possible. I never thought it could happen—not to people like us, like you and me. I wouldn't believe it—I laughed at them in the office when they said—said that times were changing. They weren't saying that—they were trying to tell me and I hardly listened. O God, how they must have laughed."

He rocked himself to and fro, half-mad, worn out. She said, steadily, "What did they say?"

"I'll tell you." He became rigid. "They said: All women are the same. All harlots, if you give them the chance. Even respectable women with grown-up daughters and a respectable husband in a respectable job—even they with their mealy mouths and their modest pretenses are the same, and their virtue lasts just as long as you watch them."

"So you watched me."

"Yes. And if I had watched you sooner it would have been better for us, all of us, because a soiled woman is no good to anyone, not even to her children, do you understand that? No good, worthless—"

"You listened to this office gossip and you spied on me."

"Yes." He was brought up short. "Yes, yes, yes! And I wish to God I had done it sooner, I—"

"You spied. What did you see? Did you see me lying naked with my lover? Did you? *Did* you?"

He was stupefied. He stared at her, silenced.

"Say you saw that too." Her face was blotchy, discolored. "Why not, when you've said so much?"

"Because I didn't," he cried, goaded. "But I saw you with him, and it wasn't for the first time, was it? Can you deny that? Can you deny you went with him—with this man whom you worship as a god?"

She did not answer. She sat with her hands clenched in her lap, with that intense rigidity he had noticed once before. We've no words left, he thought, either of us. We're burned up. But he was wrong.

"The man whom I worship as a god," she said, looking at him directly. "You are very nearly right in that one thing. Just that one thing."

"And wrong in all the others. Is that what you're saying?" He began to tremble. "Do you expect me to believe that? Do you think I'm a fool as well as a cuckold? Foolish enough to believe anything you care to tell me? Do you think I'll ever again believe *any*thing that you tell me?"

"I don't know." She leaned forward, the tensity of her body still unrelaxed. "But you have eyes. If you wish to see you can. See for yourself—there is nothing to stop you."

She got to her feet with a sudden, jerky movement that unnerved him. He could not bring himself to look at her, but he said uneasily, "Where are you going?"

She did not answer. He heard the swish of her sari and he listened, his heart hammering, but she was not going out after all. He could hear her moving about the room, the telltale sounds of her nightly routine, and he relaxed. Soon all was silent, but he waited. He did not want her to be awake when he got into bed beside her. He sat where he was, resolved not to think, and indeed his mind seemed drugged, incapable of thought; but as he dozed all that had gone came crowding back, every word and gesture hideously enlarged.

He jerked himself awake at last, and rose to his feet stiffly. A small flame was still burning before the tulasi, and he snuffed it before going in. The room was very dark; it was a little time before he could distinguish even familiar shapes in the blackness. When he did he realized that the bed was empty.

He lay down, on top of the striped coverlet. Sarojini must be in the girls' bedroom, or in Chandru's—there was nowhere else. There were no spare beds in either room—what would she be doing, sitting up? He got up quickly at that, knowing he would have no peace until he found out, and crept into the baby's room. The child was sound asleep in his cradle, breathing evenly and quietly. Huddled on the ground beside him, her head pillowed on her arm, lay Sarojini. He stood on the threshold uncertainly, looking down at her. She might be asleep, or she might be pretending sleep—he could not tell, even by listening to her breathing. It doesn't matter, he said to himself wearily, she sleeps where she wants. He went back into his room, took the coverlet off the bed, hesitated, then quickly carried it into the next room and laid it over Sarojini. Then at last he went to bed.

# 8

HE thought he would sleep at once; he had merely to lie
down, he was so tired. He did not. His overwrought mind
relived the evening, going over each word, each look,
until the whole scene was scored in fierce light against his
burning eyelids. In time it will pass as all things pass, he
said to himself in a brief moment of calm—a fragment of
detached lucidity, in between the storms; but he did not
believe it, flung himself headlong again and again into the
present, which had reality and torment. Even so he slept,
as dawn was breaking; and the meager hour he had
snatched seemed to increase rather than alleviate his exhaustion.

He woke with a sense of impending pain although he
could not yet feel it. By a curious quirk he remembered
exactly when he had last felt like this: It was in his youth,
when he had come to after an operation expecting to feel

every prick and incision made on his inert body. He had not, mercifully. This time it was different.

He got up quickly and dressed. The household was already in full swing: Sarojini in the kitchen, the maid darting in and out of the rooms, the girls laughing and talking unbearably. His head ached but he forced himself to listen, behaving normally so that they would not suspect anything was wrong. Sarojini was doing the same— avoiding his eye, addressing him no more than was necessary, yet betraying no strain. Like conspirators, in tacit accord, they efficiently set about shielding their children. And when the children had left for school there was the maid, before whom they must posture and play-act. I won't! he raged in sudden indignation. Why should I? Let her know—let the whole world know. I don't care! But he did care when he thought of his children, and the powerful urge for honesty was killed.

Automatically, he made a show of preparing for the office. At his usual time he set off. He had no intention of going there; indeed the office seemed to him an abstraction, something with which he was only vaguely connected, although he remembered quite distinctly the day before yesterday when it had had importance. Well, values altered—at least until one reached the ultimates of which religion spoke, although each man had to find out for himself what they were.

When he had reached the halfway milestone he turned

back. He knew he would have to watch and wait until Sarojini went out, then follow her, but it did not loom before him as an ordeal now as it had done the day before. One hardens, he thought, lurking in the alley, careless of the curious glances his respectability earned him; one hardens, and it is only the speed with which it happens that is left to surprise. He dwelt on this, his eyes fixed on the section of street in which his wife must emerge. Yesterday the sarcasm of a laborer had made him move; today a juggernaut would not have shifted him. He shivered at that. "Juggernaut" was an anglicization, a corruption of Jaganath, of God. He had not meant that—of course no man could withstand God. He had meant only that he had changed—changed enough to ignore the sneers of strangers.

Then he forgot side issues. Sarojini had come out, had turned and was walking up the street as she had done before. He followed closely. He could not risk losing her this time; and it did not matter whether she saw him or not. Indeed, she had invited him to see for himself. Probably, then, she knew he was following, although earlier she had seemed to take it for granted he was going to the office. Equally easily she might not suspect; for fifteen years he had gone to the office every day except for Sundays and holidays and illness, and once when he had had to look after the children, and then he had found it difficult to stay away. It doesn't *matter*, he said to himself impatiently, irritated that his mind should stray down such petty paths while the pattern of his life was being twisted out of shape. Yet he could not control it until, for an instant, he lost the green-and-red sari, and after that shock all his energies were canalized into keeping his wife in view.

Sarojini was walking quickly, despite the sun. He found it an effort to keep up with her, and was a little astonished that she, for all her slightness, showed no sign of fatigue. Well, he thought bitterly, if desire is strong enough energy can be found, so they say. He himself was sweating profusely, and physical discomfort began to edge in on his consciousness despite his anguished preoccupation. They had already covered, he surmised, something like five miles; it was a long way to come at noon— especially not knowing the way, or the end.

They were now in a winding lane, quieter than most, almost peaceful by contrast with the raucous main street off which it opened. He had never been here before, though he knew the area round about well enough; probably, he thought, because it looked more a cul-de-sac than a thoroughfare. Indeed, Sarojini had seemed to be making straight for a blank wall, and it was only as they drew near that he saw the narrow archway left in the brick. A heavy wooden door fitted the opening, and he noticed that everyone who went through closed it behind him. He did so as well, though it seemed pointless, for there was nothing beyond the gate except the continuation of an ordinary lane. Probably, he thought, the wall marked the boundary of some old rajah's domain, and to confirm him in his opinion it was more spacious here, trees in plenty, open well-tended squares, and still some traces of love and care that contrasted with the graceless indifference of erstwhile British India without.

Sarojini was walking more slowly now. In the comparative quiet he could hear the soft flip-flap of her sandals. Presently she stopped in front of a small whitewashed house, stooped for a moment to remove her sandals and went inside. Dandekar had stopped when Sarojini stopped, now he ran, his blood fevering, until he reached the house, and here he was brought to an abrupt halt. He had expected a closed door, barred to him, her husband, and he would have battered against this until his fury drew forth some reply. But there was no door; only an archway, hung with a screen that swung lightly in, out, in, out, with every puff of breeze. It seemed to mock him, that screen, moving incessantly yet never so much that he could look beyond. He seized it roughly in both hands to thrust it aside, but then he held back. Was he to go in now after his wife? Follow her in, drag her from her lover? Follow even so far as their tryst, their bed? He closed his eyes and his flesh cringed before the image. It was grotesque, unendurable, a gross and violent immodesty that the body he knew should open naked before another; yet he acknowledged that however stark his imaginings the reality would be worse.

Almost without volition his hand fell from the screen. He turned, he wanted only to get away from that house, but in his blind haste he tripped, almost falling over the sandals neatly placed before the entrance. He stared at them, small, narrow, the cheap japanned leather straps fraying at the edges—his wife's sandals, so familiar he had never really looked at them until now; and quite suddenly a vast overwhelming possessiveness took hold of him. It swept away every other emotion and consideration. Whatever he saw, whatever the cost, he would follow her in now and take her back.

She was sitting, cross-legged, on the man's right. His hand was on her bowed head, and he was murmuring to her, his voice sometimes falling to a whisper, a soft stream of indistinguishable words. In a rough circle about them sat a small group of men and women, listening—so engrossed that no one turned as he burst in. No one had even stirred; they were simply unaware of his presence.

Dandekar stood confusedly where he was. His head was swimming, rather as if he had entered some new element without preparation. His mouth was dry, full of a taste and a smell, heavy and acrid, that he knew. It's those joss sticks, he thought, looking around the walls where they hung smoking in clusters. There are too many of them. The strong smell seemed to make his other senses function erratically. He still could not hear clearly, and apart from the two central figures he could not have said what anyone in that room looked like, yet he saw with absolute precision the glowing pin point of each joss stick, the wire that held them in bundles, each minute flake of ash that floated to the floor. His sense of identity began to slip; he knew who he was—I am Dandekar, he said to himself, but the words had no reality. His knowledge of time had gone. He could not tell whether he had been standing for minutes or hours in this room full of people. A room, full of people. Quite suddenly his vision cleared, his mind began to function. He was wrong. He had followed his wife and seen for himself and he was wrong. He must get out now, at once; go out quietly, not peremptorily as he had come in, and leave his wife here until in time she came home.

He turned and tiptoed out. No one had seen him come in. No one saw him go.

# 9

HE got home like an animal, by instinct. The house was empty, except for the baby and their maid. He stared at her, frowning. He had forgotten all about her—who she was, why she was there, and it was an effort to remember. The fright in the girl's eyes recalled him to his senses. "I'm not feeling very well," he said jerkily. "I think I'l lie down for a while."

"So that's why you're home early."

"Yes. That's why I'm home early."

"You gave me quite a start." She pulled the coverlet off the bed, shook down the pillow. "There. Now what can I get you—a glass of—?"

"I don't want anything. Except to be left in peace." He spoke brusquely and was instantly sorry. The girl's eyes were soft, full of concern for him. "I'm just a bit tired," he said. "I'll be all right after I've had a little rest."

"Just you lie down. I won't let Chandru-baba make a sound, so you can sleep."

She was little more than a child in years, but she spoke with the tenderness of a woman. After all, what was he to her? An employer, who seldom if ever noticed her unless she happened to be in the way. I don't even know her name, he thought. Then he fell asleep.

When he woke, Sarojini was back, the girls were home from school, the house was in full spate again. There is no privacy in marriage, he thought, his head splitting. It's one of the things you give up, and you never realize you've given it up until something goes wrong and you want it. He lay quietly, dreading the thought of getting up and facing his wife, the maid, his talkative daughters, yet basically too honest to sham further illness. Outside he could hear them being quiet—all except the baby, and he was being hushed. They must have heard him stir, for presently the older girl came in, glancing with guarded eyes at the bed.

"I'm all right," he said to reassure her. "Just a headache. I'm getting up now."

"Oh well." There was relief in her voice, and he thought: How unnatural illness is—it frightens even children.

"Mother said to tell you, if you were awake, that dinner is ready."

"I'm coming. Tell your mother I'm having a wash."

Ramabai vanished with a swirl of her skirts. So now we're using her as a go-between, he thought wretchedly. Tell your mother; Father said to tell you. We're even descending to that. Yet he knew it had been beyond his power to call out cheerfully, "I'm coming. I won't be a minute." And Sarojini, equally, had not been able to face him.

He got up stiffly and washed under the running tap in the courtyard. The water gushed and spurted; the municipality usually manned its pumps at this hour, but for some unaccountable reason its energy dwindled by morning. It did not matter much at ground level, but when they had lived on the seventh floor it had been infuriating to watch and wait while the water trickled into the assembled containers. That was a long time ago, he thought, when we first began, and we both had more patience. Then he wondered a little that he should think of the past. It was not often that he did so, there had never been much reason for not living in the present.

Over dinner they shored up the façade, studiously avoiding each other's eye.

"Feeling better now?"

"Yes, thanks. Probably a little biliousness brought on that headache."

"Best thing to do, sleeping it off."

"Yes."

"Nalini said you looked like a crazy man," said Lakshmi. "Wild and gaping, she said."

Nalini—that must be the maid's name. "Did she?" He stared at his younger daughter, then he managed to laugh it off. "Oh well, you don't look pretty when you're ill, do you?"

"Did you have," said Sarojini, "a—a busy day at the office?"

"No. Not very busy. Chandru been good?"

"Extremely good."

About now, in their scheme of living, he usually began an account of his day. He could not do it. He turned desperately to Lakshmi.

"And what have you been learning at school today?"

"Nothing much."

He looked at the child helplessly; he could not think of a follow-up. Then Ramabai came to his rescue, and for once he was glad of her ready tongue.

"We did maths and history, then there was a talk on community projects—the man came all the way from Delhi to tell us all about them."

"Was it interesting?"

"Oh yes!" Her face lit up. "If I weren't going to be— what I'm going to be, I'd go and work in a village. They need as many people as they can get, there's so much to do."

"Is there?"

"Yes. You don't hear about it living in a town, but they're digging wells and building roads and railways and—"

He thought unsteadily, Roads, railways, bridges— that's where it all started. If I had never opened that trunk would I ever have suspected anything was wrong? And yet one would always choose to know—even with the certainty that knowledge came linked with pain. It was as if some consummately skillful unsuspected power impelled one to this extraordinary choice under the illusion of free will, and the pundits were after all right when they said that one was born to suffer for past sins. Oh well, he thought wearily, if one has sinned one must pay.

Ramabai was still talking. Despite his abstraction he noticed the maid hovering anxiously in the background. She started work in the mornings at seven, but there was no set time for her to leave; she went when she was told. Poor child, he thought, she must be longing to get home; but he could not bring himself to remind Sarojini, and it was another half hour before she remembered.

Then at last the maid was gone. Soon after nine the girls went to bed. Now the pretense can end, he thought, but the relief he had anticipated did not come. I must speak to her, he told himself, racked, but speech seemed locked somewhere beyond his dry lips, his constricted throat. He looked at Sarojini, his wife, a stranger; and quite suddenly at the same moment she looked up and their eyes met.

"I saw you today," he said simply.

She nodded, accepting the fact, offering no explanation.

"I followed you," he said. "I followed you all the way to that house and you were with him again."

She nodded once more. "Yes. I was with him."

Pain and fury were gathering inside him. He said passionately, "What were you doing? You say you, a married woman, were with this man in his house but you do not say why or what for. Am I not your husband, entitled to know? Or am I some kind of hireling gigolo to be told only as much as is good for him?"

Her eyes did not waver from his. "You are entitled to know," she said steadily. "Shall I tell you?"

He shrank back. He was suddenly, inordinately afraid of what she was going to say. Then he lashed himself. Was he to choose the idiot's way to delight, living in deliberate ignorance because he was too frightened to know? He licked his dry lips, and he said huskily, "I must know."

"Very well." Her eyes were dry, overbright with some kind of fever. "I go to be healed. So do the others whom you saw. I have a growth in my womb."

It stunned him, momentarily. He stared at her blankly, then his eyes left her face, moved down her body, while the slow realization came. A growth—a cancer: something that would grow and invade and possess body and spirit until neither was humanly recognizable. His flesh began to creep. "No," he said hoarsely, "it's not true."

"It is perfectly true."

Still he fought. This could not be happening to her, to him. "They must have made a mistake."

"No."

The finality in her voice broke him. He reached for her blindly, in an unreasoned, primitive need for something to hold on to; but she drew back.

"So now you know," she said harshly. "For a month now you've been snooping and sniffing at my heels because you suspected something very different. I've watched you, I'm not blind. You listened to every poisonous word of every petty clerk in your office and you believed it."

"No!"

"Believed every word. You've come to me—thrust yourself on me night after night after night because, God forgive you, you couldn't think of any reason for my refusal except a vicious one. *That* you believed easily enough."

"You don't know what you're saying!" he cried. "You're ill—you're—"

"You must be ill too," she said passionately. "Sick— your brain must have been sick, to have believed what you did—to have followed me as if I were a common harlot with whom you consorted but were not sure of."

He took both her hands, held them and would not let go.

"I was mad," he said. "I went mad because I loved you. Is that a crime? Is it possible to love without jealousy?"

"And without trust," she said with a deep and smoldering anger. "Is that love? Is it?"

"If only you had told me," he whispered. "Why could you not tell me?"

"Because you would have stopped me going to be healed."

"You don't know what you're saying." He shook his head, trying to clear the mists that gathered. "Stopped you being healed? I?"

"Yes, you. You would have sent me to a hospital instead. Called me superstitious, a fool, because I have beliefs that you cannot share. You wouldn't have let me be—no! You would have reasoned with me until I lost my faith, because faith and reason don't go together, and without faith I shall not be healed. Do you understand that?"

He said, speaking with difficulty, "Is he a—a faith healer?"

"Yes. You can call it healing by faith, or healing by the grace of God, if you understand what that means.

But I do not expect you to understand—you with your Western notions, your superior talk of ignorance and superstition when all it means is that you don't know what lies beyond reason and you prefer not to find out. To you the tulasi is a plant that grows in earth like the rest—an ordinary common plant. And mine is a disease to be cured and so you would have sent me to the hospital and I would have died there."

He could bear no more. She must not go on; he must stop her before they were both lost in this menacing world in which such powerful, bitter words could exist. He got to his feet, drawing her up with him. "We're both tired," he said quietly. "We mustn't go on any more . . . like this. We've been married too long, and you mean too much to me."

He expected her to resist him—and why not, he thought, with that dull ache which was the uttermost in feeling his exhausted being could now achieve; why not, since I have believed her capable of dishonoring her marriage, and our women hold nothing worse—and indeed for long dreadful seconds she stood stiffly beside him, dry-eyed, rigid. Then suddenly she yielded, shaking, leaning against him for support, tears flowing from between the tight fingers with which she had covered her face.

"I didn't mean it—" she was gasping for words, for breath, "—didn't mean what I said. Anger makes you say —strange things, but I didn't mean—how could I?—after

so long and—and our happiness, but it wasn't—wasn't
me—"

"I know." He held her, stroking her burning temples,
understanding more from these incoherent outpourings
than from the clear rock-crystal of the words she had
used before. "We mustn't say any more tonight, neither
you nor I. And you must get some sleep—it's nearly three
o'clock, did you know?"

He waited until the paroxysm was over, and then gently led her to bed.

He lay quietly on the cane easy chair and all of him
seemed dead except his mind. Paralysis, reaction, realization, panic, all had come in turn and momentarily gone.
Now he was left with the detail.

I left her to sleep on the floor, he said to himself. She
was ill and I let her lie on the floor while I slept in comfort. Pain flooded in, ebbed away leaving a dull residue.
I never knew how much it meant to her, he thought. I
never knew how much I was offending her—not once in
all these years. But she's wrong. The tulasi isn't an ordinary tree, it's a symbol; I thought I had made that clear
to her. What else did I think that wasn't so? That we were
happy? But we were happy, and we shall be happy again
when she has been cured, but she must give up this faith
healer, go to a hospital. To linger and die there, like her
mother and grandmother before. He felt himself go cold.

He had forgotten that, but now it came back to him with clarity. The older woman was shadowy, an insubstantial being who had hardly existed for him, but the other memory was floodlit. They were newly married, and they went to see her in the general ward where she had lain for six months. There was not much of her to see except her face, the rest was decently covered by white spotless sheets, even her hands; but her face was so utterly tired you knew she would never do anything again, not even die quickly because she hadn't the strength.

There was nothing for him to do. He sat idly beside Sarojini, gazing at the rows of beds in the ward. Between each burned camphor cones—to keep gnats away from the patients, the nurse said; but somehow later he knew, although nobody told him, that it was to kill the smell. The smell, he thought queerly. That's what the joss sticks were there for. He could smell them even now, here in his house. Or was it the camphor cones? He got up unsteadily. I must not be alone, he thought, I must not allow myself to feel alone. But there was nowhere for him to go. He heard the bed creak and he tiptoed in, hoping Sarojini might be awake, but she was fast asleep on her side of the double bed. She's got used to being alone, he thought, looking down at her. That's what I taught her in all these years of marriage. She was sick and frightened and she bore it alone because she did not feel she could come to me. He bent over her, his head swimming, and those overpowering odors were again in his nostrils. Almost fainting he stumbled out. The gleam of brass caught his eye and he went into the courtyard and sank down beside the tulasi. The scent of its leaves rose strongly in the night air, slowly destroying joss sticks and camphor. It was light before he went back to the easy chair.

In the morning out of hearing of the girls Sarojini said, "Are you—will you be going to the office today?"

He had not been for two days; a third would not matter. The office itself had ceased to matter. "I hadn't even thought of it," he said simply.

"There are the children."

"I know," he said wearily. "I shall go out as usual, they won't know."

Sarojini said in a strained voice, "As usual? Have you stayed away several days?"

"Only two. I shan't lose my job because of that."

As soon as he said that he knew what she was thinking. Each year the universities turned out hundreds of graduates eager for jobs . . . and one must think of the children. He said jerkily, "I don't know what—what I'm thinking of. Of course I'll go."

# 10

EVERYONE, needless to say, knew that he had been absent without leave. Kannan the peon, who regularly stayed away for three days in each month, looked at him with round puzzled eyes that asked quite plainly: How could you do such a thing? Dandekar had not believed that trivia could affect him, but his capacity for feeling seemed to be enlarging. He tightened his lips in annoyance and brushed past the peon.

As he was hanging up his coat Joseph said, with sympathy but not without some relish, "You'd better watch out—the old man's after your blood."

"Chari? Is he back?"

"No, no. The other one—the know-all Northerner."

"What did he say?"

"Nothing. He just kept bouncing in and out of his

room asking where you were. Naturally none of us knew."

"I told him you were ill," Sastri interrupted decisively. "You were, weren't you, Dandekar?"

"No," said Dandekar. "No, I wasn't ill."

"You'd better say you were." Joseph laughed. "I would, if I were in your shoes."

Dandekar toyed with the thought while he waited to go in to Ghose—who had not wasted any time in summoning him in—but he could not bring himself to it. Joseph was different; he had been brought up so strictly that now nothing but laxness was left.

Ghose's table was piled high with papers and files; he was obviously inundated with work. His mood was none too good.

"Well." He looked up at Dandekar without pity. "You were sick. I suppose that's going to be your excuse."

"No, sir."

"Have you any excuse for absenting yourself?"

Dandekar's chest began to constrict in the familiar way. He had to fight for breath.

"There were personal reasons," he managed to say.

"So you told me." Ghose's voice was cold. "Your aunt's funeral rites, if I remember correctly."

Dandekar flushed; he had forgotten that lie, and it seemed to him to be exacting his self-respect in payment.

But at least it could be nailed and remedied, and then he was through with lying forever.

"That was not the true reason," he said.

"Oh? What was?"

This has happened before, he thought, this inquisition. But I was the inquisitor. I made her go through something like this, only a hundred times worse. How did she stand it? Can there be anything left between us after this kind of torture?

"—deliberate disobedience to an order. I have no option but to fine you. Two days' pay, and five rupees." Ghose concluded his remarks.

Dandekar stared at him, his mind still wrapped in questioning. What did it feel like to be inquisitor and judge? How had he felt when he questioned Sarojini? Angered. Vindictive. Insensible with rage—otherwise he would have seen from her face how terribly wrong he was.

Ghose noted the silence, the stare; mistook it for a studied insolence, and doubled the fine. "Next time it may cost you your job," he finished. "You may go."

Dandekar stumbled out. The sudden hush that had clamped down on the office lifted.

"He's had his pint of blood, has he?" said Joseph.

"It was a little bloody," Dandekar agreed. He sat down, opening some of his neglected files.

"Bloodsucker," said Joseph, and there was an assenting murmur which Dandekar found comforting—although, again, he had not believed that such small things could touch him.

Going home with him that night Sastri said, "What did he do?"

"Two days' pay," said Dandekar, "and a ten-rupee fine."

Sastri was shocked. "Swine. He knows you're a family man. You aren't going to—to be short or anything, are you?"

"Oh no. We're all right, thank you. Sarojini's a good manager. She—"

It hit him then; he could not go on. All day he had staved her off and office, files, work and Ghose had helped; now it was beyond him.

"A cup of coffee." Sastri's voice was urgent. "Here. Come in here." He felt Sastri take his arm and went with him obediently into the small coffeehouse.

"Here you are. Drink it, it'll do you good."

He drank it, shuddering. It was black and bitter.

"It's Sarojini, isn't it? It might do you good to talk about her."

Dandekar looked up. Sastri's eyes were kind, reassuring.

"Yes," he said simply. "She has a growth in her womb."

The eyes did not move, but the kindness, the reassurance, slowly drained from them and were replaced by fear. Curiously, the other man's fear brought Dandekar back to himself. It's more than he bargained for, he thought wearily. You can't blame him, it's one of the things that are too—too mortal, to pretend about. He watched Sastri striving to regain his balance; but he did not care, one way or the other. He felt he almost knew what the other would say, to gain time.

"Are you sure?"

"That's what I asked her." He almost smiled. "Yes. She's quite sure."

Sastri broke the silence by ordering another coffee. He said stoutly, "Of course it isn't as bad as it used to be— I mean nowadays people have operations and are completely cured."

"She isn't going to have an operation."

"Why not?" Sastri spoke urgently. "She must. You must persuade her. They say delay can be—can be—is undesirable. Naturally she's frightened but—"

"I don't know whether she's frightened or not. She won't have an operation because she has no faith in it."

"But what is she going to do? Just wait and—?"

"No. She's doing something she has faith in. She's going to a faith healer."

Sastri was silent. He knew, as Dandekar knew and indeed who did not, that it was a man of some rashness and greater ignorance that inveighed against healing by faith;

yet when it came so near he was somehow uncomfortable —would have preferred to retreat rather than face the challenge.

"Of course there are faith cures," he said after a while, hesitantly, "but supposing it doesn't work? Very often it doesn't, and this isn't something for which you can keep trying one thing after another. You must speak to her— get her to see she must go to the hospital."

"She wouldn't listen and she won't go."

"You must make her." Sastri spoke decisively, firmly grounded in a society where wives obeyed their husbands. "Explain everything to her, tell her she must."

"I can't."

"My dear man, of course you can. Not right away perhaps, but in a day or two—"

"I can't! I tell you I can't." Dandekar realized he was shouting, forced himself to be calmer. "You—you don't understand. Her mother and her grandmother both— both died of the same thing, in the hospital after operations."

"That was twenty-thirty-forty years ago. A lot has changed since then."

"I know. But it has—has affected her reasoning, you can't blame her. She doesn't believe she'll—she'll recover, if she goes to the hospital."

"But you aren't just going to let her put her life in the

hands of a faith healer? After all, this is something physical, real . . . it's not like having fits. Supposing he can't cure her?"

"She believes he can."

"You'll have to talk to her. Make her see reason."

Dandekar said dully, "I can't do that. Once she sees reason she won't have any faith left . . . she said so herself. I can't risk that—I'd never forgive myself. I can't force her into the hospital either . . . I might if I were— if I could be sure, but there's no certainty even in a hospital, is there?"

"I don't know. A doctor would tell you—why don't you ask her doctor?"

"I don't know her doctor. I don't know if she's been to one."

"Then how does she know what she's got?"

"I don't know."

Sastri looked away from his friend. People in distress behaved strangely, lost their common sense, fell into lethargy, forget that life must go on. Tragedy could follow, if there was no one on hand to make them pull themselves together. He said, gently enough but firmly:

"Ask her. After that go and see the doctor, find out how serious it is. Then go to this faith healer, ask him—it doesn't matter much what you ask him but you can at least tell if he's genuine or not. When you know a little more than you do you'll be able to do something . . . to help Sarojini, do you understand?"

"Yes."

"The sooner you get it all done the better."

"Yes."

"Are you sure you—?"

"Yes," said Dandekar listlessly. "I understand. I know I look a bit stunned—I am of course, but I realize I've got to—to do something, soon. I've wasted enough time," he added bitterly, "so much energy, just in mistrusting her. I wonder why people do it? Why they can't see they're throwing themselves and their lives away?"

Sastri made no reply. He had never known Dandekar like this before—withdrawn, questioning, introspective; and he did not know, yet, quite how to take it.

# 11

THE doctor who had examined Sarojini attended outpatients at the Government Hospital between three and five in the afternoons, twice a week. It would mean having half the afternoon off, and having to ask Ghose for it. It made Dandekar feel slightly sick even to think of it, yet he dared not risk absenting himself again without permission. Perhaps for the first time in his life he thought with envy of an officer's status. A clerk must ask if he wanted to leave half an hour early, quake if he arrived half an hour late, produce a doctor's certificate if he were ill, supply whys and wherefores for every reclaimed minute of the time he had sold for a wage. An officer was free from these petty slaveries—and probably, he thought, walking to the office that morning, they never realized they were free, in the same way as he had never until now realized he was tied. It was just what one got used to.

He had spent several hours worrying over the forthcoming interview with Ghose—needlessly, it turned out. Chari was back. He had cut short his leave, feeling he had had enough rest, in much the same way as he ended his inspection tours when there was nothing left to inspect. Dandekar felt almost lighthearted with relief. It was the first bit of luck he had had for—for a long time, he said to himself. It had been a long month of disaster.

Just before lunchtime, with the morning mail dealt with, and as much of the accumulations cleared as was possible, he went to see Chari.

"Sir, would you please grant me two hours' leave this afternoon?" He had rehearsed this.

Chari looked up. It was not Kannan, and it was not Joseph, determined lotus-eaters both. It was, surprisingly, Dandekar.

"Of course, my dear chap," he said absently, and went back to his files.

"Thank you, sir. Thank you very—very much."

All his clerks introduced a fervent note into their thanks when they got what they wanted; but there was an undercurrent of hysteria in Dandekar's voice that made Chari glance up at him.

"I should—um—take the afternoon off," he said, casually enough, wondering what could have produced such severe signs of stress. "It's hardly worth while coming back to the office for an hour."

Then he sent for Ghose.

When Ghose came Chari said, "Do you know what's wrong with Dandekar?"

"Is something wrong with him?"

"He looks wretched. He came in here a few minutes ago wanting a couple of hours off—"

"Did you sanction it?" The interruption was forceful, explosive.

Chari looked up at Ghose with surprise. "Yes. In fact I told him to take the afternoon off. Wouldn't you have?"

"No," said Ghose with cold anger. "Not unless he had some very adequate reason. Did he give any?"

"My dear chap," said Chari, irritated, "one just doesn't question a man when he looks like that!"

"I don't know what he looks like," began Ghose. "He deliberately—"

"Then perhaps you ought to make it your business to find out," suggested Chari.

Ghose went out. He was too good a civil servant, trained and disciplined, to argue with his chief, but the encounter rankled. These bloody Southerners, he thought resentfully, they all hang together. . . .

Dandekar was in the Government Hospital outpatients' waiting room at five minutes to three. The room was a large one, but it was already full. Early arrivals sat on a wooden bench along the wall, the rest on the floor. A veranda outside took the overflow.

Dandekar tried not to look at anyone—partly because he was a healthy man with a healthy man's aversion to illness, partly because he had developed an inverted hypersensitivity which made him feel diseased himself, dreading the curious eye. Yet when he did look, as he could not help doing eventually, there was nothing to be seen. People were decently fleshed, decently clothed. It's when they go in that other room, he thought, behind that screen, it's different. Then he became conscious of the smell. Not joss sticks this time—he shivered. Something else, hospital smell. An emanation of flesh and blood and the secret exudings of human beings, distorted but hideously alive under the sprays and washes they put out to kill it. Like an animal whose slaughter has been bungled. It nauseated him. He could feel his whole body contracting, drawing back into some dim memory of protective shell that it had not for aeons possessed.

He nearly missed his turn, he was so obsessed. A neighbor nudged him, and he stumbled to his feet, got to the screen, was behind it. There were two women there, one a nurse, the other a doctor in a white coat bent over a basin scrubbing her hands.

"What is the trouble?"

"It's my wife. She—"

The doctor turned, exasperated. These bloody Southerners and their prudish imbecilities! It was less common now, but not unknown, for women patients to seek medical aid at one remove. The doctor had no patience with such practices.

"If it's your wife," she said, "she ought to have come, not you."

"She—she did. She came to—to see you and—and—"

He was stammering, coherence of speech and thought impaired by brusqueness.

"Sit down." The doctor was not inhuman, despite her professional training. "What is wrong with your wife?"

"She has a growth." He was sweating, but he could speak. "You advised an operation. I just want to know—"

"What the chances of recovery are." They all wanted to know that. It was a reasonable question, and reasonable to be put twice, for truth had its variation, as between patient and relative. "Name?"

"Dandekar."

"Wife's name?"

"Sarojini."

The nurse was riffling through the filing cabinet. It was like the ones they had in the office, except that it was painted white. The system of labeling was similar too. It shocked him a little that lives should be filed and indexed like office correspondence; it reminded him of one of Joseph's stories, that if you died in the hospital they filed your body away in lockers that were marked from A to Z, and that was where your relatives found you. He found the story easier to believe now.

"Here we are." The doctor was studying the case sheet. "Did you say cancer?"

He had not actually said it; he had meant it. He nodded wordlessly.

"No, no. Not a cancer, an innocent tumor, quite common in women. I'm sure I explained that to her. But she ought to have it out because of the symptoms."

"What symptoms?"

"These hemorrhages."

"I didn't know," he said huskily. "She didn't tell me."

"I expect she didn't want to frighten you." The doctor glanced at her watch. She did not want to be on her feet half the night as well as all day, which she certainly would be at this rate. We forget they're human beings, she thought. They repay us the compliment.

"This way." The nurse moved forward starchily. Dandekar did not even hear her. He said, "If she will not have the operation?"

"She ought to. Neglect in these cases is always dangerous."

"Only one—one more question. Is it a serious operation?"

"It's an abdominal operation." She spoke automatically. "All abdominal operations are major operations."

If she had not been in public service, constantly working against time, drained of vitality by the ceaseless, swollen flow of sufferers—if she had been in private practice where people came singly in cars and even the standard euphemisms wore plush—she might have added that it was a convenient classification, no more; that a great many women underwent abdominal operations and survived, and quoted statistics to illustrate it. But there was no time for all this. Moreover, she thought, it's a safe formula; if it does go wrong they can't turn around afterwards and accuse you.

Dandekar got up to go. "She won't have it," he said bleakly.

The doctor shrugged. Fools, she thought without rancor, anachronisms that should have gone with the Middle Ages. But she had not the time to say so, and it was really not her job.

Chari had told him not to come back, and if he went home he would be early, would have to think up some story for Sarojini even if she didn't ask. Dandekar walked slowly away from the hospital, wondering how to kill the hour, dreading to spend it alone and have his thoughts catch up on him, yet with nowhere to go. The two halves of his life had so far made up a satisfactory whole, and unlike many of his friends he had no inconsequent intermediate platforms onto which he could climb to escape the more vicious onslaughts of thought. The child provided one.

He had been trailing Dandekar for some time, this rag-

ged street Arab, had noted the strained face, the irresolute walk, had weighed up his general air of respectability
against the compulsive needs he had learned men had, and
interpreted the signs as favorable. He sidled up behind
Dandekar and discreetly twitched his sleeve.

The boy was about the age of his younger daughter,
the same size, otherwise Dandekar would have understood
sooner. As it was he merely, and quite gently, shook off
the interfering hand. There was nothing he wanted, and he
did not think anyone could help him. There it came again,
that hand, and this time it clung. Dandekar stopped
abruptly and turned. To his surprise the boy, instead of
retreating, boldly stood his ground, and as their eyes met
he began to smile—a sly, conspiratorial and ingratiating
smile which Dandekar's mind correctly interpreted and
instantly rejected. He was not a stupid man, nor a naïve
one; yet some streak of illogical purity in his make-up
precluded him from too easily believing that this child
who was like his daughter could be a pimp.

"Nice woman, sir. Help you." Again the shady smile.

"Help me? Do you think anyone can?"

"Yes, sir. Nice woman, please you much." The boy's
voice grew urgent, detecting signs of wavering. He raised
both hands, and Dandekar saw that the first two fingers
of his left hand tightly locked the forefinger of his right.
Then he understood.

Something was wrong. He felt he ought to be shocked

and in a way he was; yet he found he could not take his eyes from those thin, explicit fingers. It held him, the lewdness of those innocent hands, created a fever in his blood that sent it throbbing and erratic through his veins. He knew it could not be contained; and at last he drew a long breath and said simply, "Where?"

He felt emptied, derelict, lying beside the woman. The moments of oblivion were done with. At any second now his mind would take over, the triumphing, imperious body once more fall under its control. He waited quite calmly, thinking: It will be bad; I must try to remember how powerful it was, how irresistible, otherwise it will be unbearable.

The withdrawal was mental now, as well as physical. The woman realized it and rose, standing with her back to him while she wound her cloth about her, twisted her long hair into the tight knot from which it had come loose. He watched her, trying to recapture what it had been like, but it was useless. Now it began, the slow quelling of the body. I must have been mad, he thought. What made me do it? How could I at a time like this? Now? With that hospital smell still on me? He stared down at himself with widening eyes, then up at that naked unknown back; and turning suddenly she caught him unawares.

"Don't look like that." She spoke with rough sympathy.

"You're not the first husband that's wanted a change. It's natural. Nothing to it."

He looked at her mutely. It was not natural. She did not know what she was saying. How could she, unless he told her? He thought he would tell her, felt his mind clawing at the possibility of relief this offered, but he saw she had lost interest and was waiting for him to go. He got up quickly, felt in his pocket and handed her a note without looking at it. Then he went out.

He had nearly reached home when he realized he was still going to be a quarter of an hour early. It had all been done in well under an hour.

When he got home Sarojini was not in. The place seemed pale and chill, like an unlit lamp. For a moment or two he stood in the courtyard, thinking: This is what it will be like, always, when she is gone. He could not accept the thought. It's impossible, he said to himself. She's not going to die, the doctor said it was something quite common in women, curable— He stopped. In the confused horror of that hospital he had not fully grasped what the doctor had said, comprehending only that his wife's life was in danger. Now it came to him that what Sarojini had was not cancer, and that it could be cured; and it was like moving from some malevolent sphere into those human, more tenable realms where hope still dwelt.

Not cancer, he repeated to himself, not cancer. He

paced up and down the courtyard while he waited for his wife, cradling this thought alone among the encroaching hordes, and aware of something near to excitement. At last he heard her step, the rustle of her clothes. He waited, trembling, until she had slipped off her sandals and come in, then he almost ran to her and took her hands.

"It's not cancer," he said eagerly. "You must have misunderstood. The doctor—" It had slipped out, where he had been; but Sarojini didn't seem to notice or mind.

"Cancer?" She stared at him. "What made you think it was?"

"You said a growth."

"It is. They call it innocent."

She drew a long breath, and her face seemed to change; the lines upon it grew, the shadows deepened in violence. With his new unfolding awareness he knew what it was like for her; even, momentarily, physically felt her pain. The sense of relief he had known began to slip away, but he clung tenaciously to the few precious grains that remained.

"It's innocent and it's curable," he said stubbornly. "The doctor said so. She said if you had the operation now—"

"No."

"Why not? You must—you must be cured. I can't—"

"I will be cured, in my own way."

"By this—this faith healer?"

"Yes. I have faith in him and he will cure me." She spoke deliberately, strangling the protesting words that were already forming in his brain. There's nothing I can do, he thought, frozen, helpless. I can't move, I'm trapped. She must go on alone along her way and if anything happens— Oh well, he thought wearily, what guarantee of safety is there in any of the ways we take? It was a strange thought, new to him. Death had always been remote, always applicable to other people; until now it had never been acknowledged a near neighbor.

"The girls are coming." She broke in on his preoccupation.

"I can hear them." He managed to smile. The thunder they made pounding the bare iron stairs was formidable. Yet their voices from their usual playground on the roof had been, he realized, equally loud, and he had hardly heard them. Some kind of capsule seemed to have formed about him, through which the world had come filtered and faint. Now it rapidly dissolved. He could hear in varying volume the seven families above, the cries of their children, the homecomings of the men; and in the court-yard the tap began its rhythmic evening thud-thud-thud.

The show was over, at last they were in bed and the darkness was blessed. If only one could cut off one's mind as easily, he thought, staring up at the black line of cord that suspended a bulb over the middle of their bed. But the strain of supporting the evening, the exhausting days, were already blanking his mind, and in a few minutes he was asleep.

It was a deep, sound sleep, dreamless and thoughtless, or if there had been any they were gone without trace when he woke. I must have been tired, he thought, to sleep like that. Or maybe it was the woman and she did help as the boy said. The woman. My God, he thought, gazing up into the blinding darkness that was not even flecked with dawn, what sort of a beast am I to have lain with a whore while my wife was so ill? To have come from her and slept like this without a care for my wife? To have pandered to lust at such a time? He got up, his peace in splinters, and went outside intending to lie in the easy chair where his restlessness would not disturb Sarojini.

It was wet with evening dew. He got out a cloth and wiped the wooden frame dry, then he realized that the cane was soaked. He went back to the bedroom, but there was nowhere to sit except on the bed and he was not even sure that he could sit still. He groped around for something to take the chill off the stone floor, and at length he took the striped coverlet laid across the foot of the bed and spread it and sat down with his knees drawn up and his back against the wall. It seemed comfortable, for the first few minutes; after that he found that he had to keep on changing position and finally even that did not help. At length he opened the coverlet full length and lay down on it on the floor, his limbs aching. This is what Sarojini had to do, he thought with the thrust of guilt like a knife in his side. She lay on the floor and I let her and she was ill and—my God, my God, he thought, his head near to bursting, maybe she was bleeding and I slept in comfort on the bed and didn't even think what it was like for her, I just let her lie on the floor. He dozed off at last with this thought uppermost and was roused about an hour later by the cries of his son which he thought were Sarojini's. I must cover her, he thought confusedly, she's cold, she's bleeding—

"What is the matter?"

Sarojini's voice pushed him into full consciousness. He realized he was standing in a corner of the room, half entangled in the coverlet and clutching it desperately in both hands.

"Nothing. The boy startled me, that's all," he answered automatically, and he thought with sudden illumination of that dark night, I did go to cover her; I took her the coverlet and I remember laying it over her. It was like a stray cold current of resuscitating air on a suffocating monsoon night.

# 12

SATURDAYS were half-days, so that Dandekar was spared the ordeal of having to ask once again for leave when he went to visit the man his wife had so much faith in. After that—what? Dandekar had no idea. Sastri had suggested the plan and he had fastened onto it like a leech because it offered some kind of action when stand-still was torture.

"I told you," said Sastri patiently. "It'll give you a chance to find out if he's genuine or not. That's the first step."

"How will I know?" Dandekar spoke simply, like a child. If the issue had been lesser, lighter, the easy boast of the worldly man would have come: "I'll watch out, never fear; he won't be able to put anything over on me. If he's a trickster it'll stick out a mile even before he starts—it always does." Now all he could utter was truth.

"How will you know?" Sastri was pulled up short by the unbecoming question. The issue was big in his eyes too, but it was not personal. He said, "My dear man, of course you'll know. Just listen to what he has to say and if he's a charlatan he's bound to give himself away."

"If he did I wouldn't know."

"Of course you would."

"Would you?"

"Anyone would."

Dandekar had no notion of trapping his friend. He said with the same terrifying simpicity, "Will you come with me? I'm certain I won't be able to tell."

Sastri recoiled. Healing by faith, the performance of the impossible, the revelation of the divine, mystery and beatitude—all these coursed in his blood, were a part of his inheritance from a country that looked inward in its quest for light. He could not deny it, and he did not wish to; yet he felt quite clearly, though loath to clothe it in words even to himself, that he did not want to be involved. These things existed and he existed, side by side without conflict.

"Will you?" Dandekar waited patiently.

"I promised to take my wife," Sastri spoke rapidly, "take my wife out. Otherwise, my dear fellow, I would certainly have come with you, you know that."

So Dandekar went alone.

He had not reckoned on the house being empty. Extraordinary possibilities had come to him in shoals, but none of the commonplace had even glanced him by.

He wandered through the empty rooms, at a loss. Nothing had been either packed away or stored. In the courtyard were incense, camphor, a jar of oil; in an open box nearby the silver censers, the small hand bell, the rose-water sprinklers that were used during pujas. In one of the rooms was a tin-lined teak chest, half full of rice. On the terrace, on a mat, prepared fruit—figs, dates, sweet lime, tamarind—were drying in the sun. He came down again, wondering that no single window or door was locked, then he recollected where he was. To come here in anything but simplicity would be sacrilege. No one would.

"What is it you want?"

The voice startled him; it seemed to come from under the staircase. He peered underneath, and in the shadows thought the man was kneeling, but it was a dwarf.

"You woke me up thumping about the place like that," the dwarf grumbled, emerging into the light. "What do you want?"

He stared up at Dandekar, head thrown back, eyes yellowish-brown in a clay-colored face and expressionless. Dandekar, embarrassed, found it impossible to meet those eyes, so far below the level of his own. He said awkwardly, looking nowhere, "I came here to see—"

"To see him, I suppose. They all do, even the blind, night and day, when he's here. Nobody comes when he's not."

"I didn't know he was not here. Where is he?"

"Where should he be? In his village, of course."

"When will he come back?"

"Who can tell with the Swami? In his own good time I daresay, not yours."

"In a few days?"

"Maybe days. Maybe weeks."

The plan was disintergrating. What was he to do now —nothing except wait? It was intolerable.

"Go to the village, if it's that bad." The dwarf's voice seemed to mock him. "That's what the rest of 'em do, heaven help their miserable bodies, and you're no better than the rest, are you?"

"I can't." Dandekar anxiously strove to justify himself. "I work in an office, I might lose my job if I—"

"Well, if you can't you can't. Pity, isn't it?" The dwarf yawned and walked away, moving with the bowlegged gait of an obese child. Dandekar followed.

"This village—how far is it? Can I get there in a day?"

"Not today, you can't. You've got to cross a river, and the ferry doesn't ply except mornings."

"Tomorrow then. How long will it take?"

"Depends how quickly you walk—how quickly the bullocks walk, if you go by cart."

"By train?"

"There's no train goes there."

"Bus, then."

"There's no bus goes there either."

Dandekar was appalled. He was a second-generation city dweller, with the unconsious creed that no two points could exist that were not linked by mechanical means. One might not choose to use them, but they were there. He was ready to give up then. The practical difficulties were too great, and apart from that, in prudence one did not pit one's wits against fate, if it seemed set against action. God's will be done. But the dwarf intervened.

"What's the matter? Can't you walk, you've got two legs?"

"Yes, of course." Dandekar drew a long breath. "I'll walk."

He went slowly out, but at the slatted screen he turned and faced the dwarf, this time looking directly into his eyes.

"I've got two legs," he said. "What you've got is a tongue as sour as turned milk."

He relished saying that; it was repayment in part for the battering he had received. But later came qualms about baiting the dwarf.

Dandekar had given himself three hours to cover the six miles to the river, but he had miscalculated. The route lay across country, and his city feet could find neither rhyme nor rhythm in the rolling, unruly lie of the land. He blundered on, painfully aware of flint and earth and stubble under the thin soles of his sandals, stooping frequently to clear the dust that collected maddeningly between his toes. How did they do it? He watched a file of peasants go by—and they were carrying loads, and their feet were bare. Well, he tried to console himself, perhaps they cannot do what I do. But here under the wide-open sky, letters and figures lost all meaning like sounds in the distance; it was the earth, one's capacity to bear it, that was something of value.

He had risen at four that morning. An early train, half-awake, clanking and slow, had brought him at five to the carven granite pillars that marked the city's boundaries. It was half-past seven now, and the river was still nowhere in sight.

"How much farther to the river?" he had to shout, for already the file of workers was well ahead of him, keeping up that curious lilting pace which Europeans called the coolie-trot.

"The river?" The tail end turned. "Not far. Not at all far."

Dandekar's heart sank at the encouraging note he detected. The man had seen he was tired and was trying to cheer him on, minimizing distance to do so. They all did it, but country people were the worst, telling you not what you wanted to know but what they thought you might like to hear. Dandekar detested the habit; his part-Western mind fought against alleviations which his part-Eastern mind occasionally hinted might be wise. Now he had no idea of how far he had to go. He kept doggedly on. Once he had decided to do something he did not easily give up. And besides—he conceded the point wryly—at this stage it was easier to go on than to go back.

It was close on nine when he reached the river, a wide expanse of gray-green water between clay and mud flats. A number of people were waiting on either shore, and so was the ferry, an affair of tree trunks lashed together with hemp and manned by a single boatman. Dandekar sat down to wait, though he could see no reason for it. When he ventured to ask, the boatman said briefly, "Currents," and pointed to the stagnant water. An air of unreality descended on Dandekar. Was it really he, Dandekar, a senior clerk in the service of the goverment of India, sitting in white dhoti and sober black coat on the banks of the river among half-naked farmers and fishermen?

"Hey you, sir! Are you coming?"

Dandekar squelched across the mud and got on the ferry, on which the rest of the company had already assembled. Then he had to close his eyes. It seemed such a makeshift affair, and the water was terrifyingly close, endowed with an unsuspected power whose suck and strain he could now clearly feel as they pulled away from the shore. In midstream it seemed easier; there was a short lull in which they seemed hardly to move and he thought the worst was over, but in the same instant the raft swung violently, caught in cross tides, throwing him against his neighbor.

"Don't worry, sir." It was the boatman, his body running with sweat but calm enough. "It's often a bit rough here."

"Is it always as bad as this?"

"This is nothing." The man spat betel juice into a whirlpool. "You should see it when the river's in spate. But there's some fools want to cross it even then—mostly the Swami's fools—think he gives them some kind of protection."

"If the Swami were with me," someone spoke up, "I'd feel safe enough whether the river was in spate or not."

"In that case I daresay you would be safe," said the boatman. "It's panic that starts disaster, mostly. Why, I remember once on the Ganges—during the Mahamagam festival this was—and there wasn't a breath of wind either . . ."

The tactless story ended, with the loss of a hundred pious lives, as they reached the other shore. Dandekar scrambled out, paid the ferry, and was once more at a loss. His action, he perceived, seemed to proceed in sections. Once launched he could move without too much difficulty to the end, but there he had to stop and gather his strength afresh, to map out and negotiate the next stretch.

"Are you looking for the Swami?"

It was one of the passengers, whom he had taken for a fisherman from the breechcloth he wore and the blackness of his skin, but his speech was otherwise.

"How did you know I was?"

"What else would you be doing here?"

Dandekar had to smile. What else, in this desert beyond a river?

"As a matter of fact I am. Can you tell me where he lives?"

"He doesn't live anywhere in particular. Usually under a tree or in the nearest hut if it rains."

"Can you tell me where that is? And how far?"

"About a quarter of a mile. Follow the path and you can't go wrong."

Dandekar looked around. There was a path, well defined, that he had missed in his general confusion. Hundreds of people must come this way, he thought; the earth was packed tight under his feet, mud and stones welded by pressure into something approaching a fair road surface. There was no need to ask his way now. He had merely to follow the path and would come to the Swami. And what then? I'll think about that when I come to it, he said to himself. It was a new philosophy with him, a month old. Before that he had been wont, like a prudent householder, to look ahead, to think and plan not only for the next day but for the next year and even the years to come. That, however, was in the days when he had been able to base his plans upon certainties—even if, again in the name of prudence, not one of these plans but was preceded by the phrase "God willing."

# 13

THE path led to a small village no different from any other with its squares of green paddy, its palms, its thrifty patches of bean and pumpkin vine, of eggplant and lady's-finger. And there on the dung-washed porch of a mud-walled hut he found the Swami. He was sitting by himself —though at no great distance squatted a number of his followers—gazing into the sunshine.

The man had been so elusive, the way to him so far-flung and winding, that now he was actually upon him Dandekar could hardly believe it. He stood where he was, uneasily considering whether to advance, ask private audi-ence of this total stranger, question him as Sastri had sug-gested (but the suggestion seemed both impertinent and extremist now); above all, unsure of his ability to do any of these things.

Hardly aware of him the villagers placidly went about their work. I suppose they've got used to strangers, he thought. I suppose they get all kinds. The steady thwack of an ax somewhere overhead took his attention, and looking up he saw a man felling the topmost palm fronds, sending them swishing to earth like giant green feathers. Presently the man slithered down, and Dandekar said (though his face was engraved on his memory), "Is that the Swami?"

"Yes. That one there, on the porch."

"What is he doing?"

"Doing? He isn't doing anything." The man sounded surprised, as if he had been asked what a tree was doing; and it came to Dandekar, with something of a shock, that perhaps it was his firm grounding in a city that made him assume that one must always be doing something. This fresh outlook enabled him to stay where he was for a while without chafing, then advance and take his place among the Swami's followers, still without fretting.

It was a beautiful morning, he thought, looking about him; but he had to admit he had no real means of comparison. In the day's rush, unless it was raining heavily enough to earn a curse, he hardly ever noticed what the mornings were like. Evenings were different. He had time to spare, and walking back from the office he often lingered, despite the call of his wife and home, to watch the beautiful cadences of the dying day, the spectacular beauty of some violent sunset. Office and home. Wife and home. That's why I'm here, he thought with a jolt. What's the matter

with me—sitting here in the sunshine thinking about sun-
sets, letting everything else go? He stood up, indignant
with himself, meaning to march up to the Swami, but at
the same moment the Swami rose, almost as if he had anticipated the move, and beckoned him forward. Dandekar froze where he stood. All his previous misgivings
returned, he would gladly have sat down again, merged
in the assembly; but now hands, voices, were urging him
on, he had no choice but to proceed. No choice whatever,
he said to himself, and he walked slowly forward between
the waiting people and up the porch to the Swami. He
must have swayed a little then, perhaps from lack of sleep,
the unaccustomed sunlight, for he felt a hand steadying
him, guiding him into the cool inner room, and he went
docilely and with gratitude.

He could not have said, afterwards, how long in reality
he sat there. By the clock, perhaps twenty minutes; but
he had no inclination to check his time sense by looking at
his watch. On a narrow mat, his back against the wall,
sat the Swami doing nothing as before, but very tranquil;
even his hands were still. The stillness crept into Dandekar too. Somewhere, remotely, was the thought that he
had no time to waste, that the ferry stopped working at
midday, and that there was a river to cross by then . . .
but it rested quietly, without querulousness, and perhaps,
he thought, perhaps we are foolish to allow ourselves to

be driven frantic by thought. He waited without impatience, and presently the Swami said, so quietly as hardly to break the silence:

"You are in trouble?"

"Yes."

"You yourself?"

"No. My wife."

"You think I can help her?"

"Yes." Dandekar drew a long breath, forced himself to think. "She believes in you, she comes to you . . . you can stop her coming."

"Why?" It was gently asked, the voice of a questioning elder dealing with a lovable if wayward child.

Dandekar knew the answer; but now with those quiet eyes on his he found it extraordinarily difficult to speak.

"Because she is ill," he stammered. "She must go to the hospital . . . have an operation, she must . . ." His voice trailed away, and in the silence he felt another question crystallizing, almost as if the Swami had spoken: In what way did the Swami prevent Sarojini from entering the hospital?

"I know you don't—don't stop her," he answered the unvoiced question, "but if you weren't there—" He stopped again, aware of yet another question forming in the silence: And where else should the Swami be? Dead —in hiding—for the sake of one woman?

"I don't mean that," he began again. "But if perhaps

you—you refused to see her—she would have no option but the hospital and . . ." His voice died away. It's not possible, he thought. I'm asking the impossible. How can he refuse to see her? He lives in the open, even his house has no locks. Dandekar had no more to say. The silence prolonged itself, and how long it lasted he could not tell. It was the Swami who finally broke it.

"If you wish your wife to be treated in the hospital why do you not tell her so?"

"I have. She won't listen."

"If you insisted?"

"She'd go, I suppose." He drew a long breath. "But you can't force people, can you? At least one shouldn't. In a crisis like this they've got to make their own decisions. . . . It wouldn't be fair otherwise, would it?"

The Swami did not answer. And why should he, Dandekar thought, it's his case I've been making. Then with a sudden flare of Sastri's suspicions he thought, He's been putting words into my mouth, he's got me to say the things he wanted, he's as clever as a monkey, as they all are. He looked up abruptly, challenging the Swami, but the serene face before him did not change. It was a narrow face, thin, pale, with that luminous quality of too little flesh making visible the white bone beneath skin—the face of a consumptive, a saint, a starving pauper. But not, thought Dandekar, the face of a clever monkey.

He rose to go. The Swami did not move, but as Dandekar reached the threshold said, without emphasis, with tranquillity, "If you wish you can help."

For a second or two Dandekar did not understand. Then he saw the small leather pouch, open, that hung from a nail in the lintel with copper and silver coins reposing in it. All his lulled suspicions awoke, jostling for his attention, but while the clamor was at its height the Swami said again, "If you wish." Slowly, then, he took some money out and without looking at it placed it in the pouch, which swung and swayed freely from its anchoring nail.

When he came out he realized that a lot of time had gone by—much more than he had intended—and there was a danger of missing the ferry. If he did he would have to wait until the next day, with the probability of arriving late at the office. Dismay filled him at the thought—although not so long ago the matter had been of no moment, the office another life, unconnected with him. He began walking faster; toward the end he was running.

He reached the river in time to see the raft neatly berth on the opposite shore. He called loudly, but his voice did not carry across that expanse of water, or the boatman preferred not to hear it. It was his last trip for the day; and with a sinking heart Dandekar saw his ebony body silhouetted idly against the midday sun.

# 14

SASTRI looked aghast at him when he walked into the office at half-past ten on Monday morning.

"Really, Dandekar!" he exploded, whispering so that the junior clerks at their distant desks should not overhear. "Whatever on earth possessed you?" Then quickly, remembering, "Is everything all right—at home?"

"Yes, more or less," said Dandekar, frantically pulling out ledgers, files, papers, in a gallant attempt to make up leeway.

"Then what happened to you?"

"It's a long story." Dandekar bent over his work. "Later—I'll tell you later."

"Bet your life his nibs will want to hear it." It was Joseph, first to recover from the awe in which the others were still engulfed—the respectful awe of timid men for intrepid ones, however foolish.

"If he wants to hear it I'll tell him the whole—"

"Dandekar." It was Ghose's voice, Ghose was standing in the doorway. Dandekar rose, and the sentence went unfinished.

"You may not be aware of it," said Ghose, heavily sarcastic, "but this office starts functioning in the morning—not the afternoon."

Dandekar's mouth hardened at the sarcasm. He had meant what he said. If Ghose had asked he would have poured out the whole story—certainly some of it. Now he merely said, formally, "I'm sorry, sir. I was unavoidably detained."

"I see." Ghose stared coldly at the clerk. He knew what he would have done—sacked the man, or at least severely reprimanded him; after all one couldn't run an office without discipline. But there was Chari, whose special pet this man seemed to be; and he schooled himself to say, as formally as Dandekar, but icily, "In future will you kindly avoid these unavoidable occurrences?"

Dandekar went out, mortified, hurt, but less angry than he might have been. He doesn't know, he thought. If he knew, would he pile more trouble onto me? Would any human being, unless he were perverted?

He bent over his work once more, and the others, seeing the graven mask he had fitted over his emotions, knew he was hard pressed and on the whole forbore to probe further.

Most of the clerks brought their lunch with them, packed by their wives in aluminum lunch carriers. The alternative was to eat in the coffeehouse, which provided quick-fried snacks, or to send the peon down to bring something back.

Dandekar had not gone home after leaving the village. He had caught the first ferry and come straight on. Now hunting through his coat pockets—with the peon's guileless eyes following every movement—he realized the last of his money had gone to pay the ferryboat man.

"I've changed my mind," he said brusquely, dismissing Kannan. "I'll go down myself a bit later." He sat down again at his desk, and at once his appetite doubled its demand. I'll get Sastri to lend me enough for a meal, he thought, though even minor borrowing was against his nature; but Sastri relieved him of the trouble.

"What about tiffin, Dandekar?" he said, bustling in. "Kannan said you were going down for a meal and that was a quarter of an hour ago. This won't do at all you know, you must eat."

"Yes I know," said Dandekar weakly. "The fact of the matter is—you see Sarojini didn't—"

"Well if she didn't pack your tiffin box you'll have to eat in the restaurant," said Sastri briskly. "Come on now."

*144*

"Actually I"—Dandekar swallowed and the words resisted utterance—"don't feel much like food."

"My dear chap, come with me." Sastri took command, grasping him firmly by the arm.

Opening off the main office was a small room used for storing empty cardboard boxes and the gunny sacks in which confidential wastepaper was baled for pulping. In some curious way this room had become the clerks' sanctum, whose sanctity the officers hardly invaded at all, or only with due circumspection. There was a long deal packing counter, ideal for meals, a sink in one corner with running water, and several ramshackle chairs of varying height urged into some sort of conformity by identical khaki-colored cushions. As a room it had the curious comfort of shabby old age.

It was empty now; Sastri had seen to it that it was. He pushed Dandekar into a chair and sat himself down, drawing both chairs up to the counter on which reposed his tiffin carrier.

"Look here, Dandekar," he said in what was nearly a hectoring tone, "I know you're upset and have been for several weeks. But it won't help if you starve. Now there's enough here for both of us—look for yourself. My wife's got the right idea—she doesn't believe in skimping on food."

He began taking down the aluminum containers,

stacked neatly on top of each other in the carrier, naming the contents of each as he did so. "Rice, curds, pickle, dhal, and—ah, this is excellent—lime-and-rice. I recommend that, my wife makes excellent lime-rice."

Dandekar's pride gave way. He was hungry, and Sastri had a way with him. He had it in more ways than one, for afterwards Dandekar found himself relating the whole of his experiences.

"So he wouldn't make any promises," said Sastri, when Dandekar had finished.

"Well, I wouldn't say that," said Dandekar with painful accuracy. "I didn't exactly ask him to make any."

"Nor did he give any kind of undertaking to leave Sarojini alone."

"No, he didn't. But he isn't the one who—anyway I didn't ask him for an undertaking."

"I don't know what you *did* ask him. You spent hours closeted with him and—"

Dandekar was silent. He would have said more or less the same things, had positions been reversed. Yet he did not know how to explain what had happened. In words it sounded bald, simple, even stupid, but there was no other medium than words in which to communicate its spirit, and that was the heart of the matter.

"What did you *make* of the man?" Sastri's insistence

broke through his abstraction. "Is he a charlatan? Is it possible that he's genuine?"

"I don't know," said Dandekar slowly. "I don't think he's a charlatan. There were a good many people there . . . would they have been there if he was?"

"But your own impression?"

"I don't know," cried Dandekar, putting his head in his hands. "There are so many impressions, one on top of the other. If you had asked me there in that village I would have answered without hesitation, but afterwards one always has second thoughts and just now I couldn't help remembering about the money—"

"What money? Did you give him money? Did he ask for it?"

"He didn't actually ask. If I hadn't wanted I needn't have given any—"

"You did, though."

"Yes."

"That's why you're short," said Sastri, inspired. "Why you haven't been able to buy yourself a meal though anyone with half an eye can see you're famished."

"It wasn't only that." Dandekar flushed. "I've had other—expenses, I didn't have much money to take in the first place, and there was the ferry to pay."

"It's a bad sign." Sastri, his mind on another track, had hardly heard what he said. "The genuine ones never take money. If he has done he's a—" Sastri stopped, aware of a faint tremor somewhere warning him to be careful. One never knew what power these men might have; there were certainly plenty of people who would vouch for it.

"It doesn't prove he's not genuine," he amended. "It's just that generally speaking, it's not too favorable a sign."

"I know."

"And you really have no idea what to make of the man."

"No."

"Not even now, thinking things over."

"No."

They both sat quiet after this, finishing their meal in silence. What to do next, although never very clear, had hinged on the establishment of this crucial point. Dandekar's overwrought, Sastri thought. If I—or any other man of average intelligence—had gone of course I'd have been able to tell what was going on, whether it was all a fraud. And Dandekar thought, a faint resentment rising in him: Would he have been able to tell any better than I?

Sastri said, rinsing the empty containers under the tap, meticulously swishing stray grains of rice down the sink:

"What will you do now?"

"Let Sarojini go her own way. I've fought as far as I know how—I just don't know what to do next."

Sastri turned, water dripping from his wet hands onto

*148*

his dhoti unnoticed. "You can't just stand by," he said decisively. "If the man's a rogue you can't leave your wife in his hands—you'll have to get her away by hook or by crook."

But he had no suggestions to offer.

# 15

DANDEKAR had meant exactly what he said: Sarojini would have to continue seeing the Swami because he did not know how to stop her. Did he want to? He was not sure. He saw her come back from him tranquil once more, anxiety over her sickness stilled—perhaps even her pain eased. He asked her once, and she answered, hesitantly, "I don't know . . . all I know is I feel better every time I go to him. While I'm there I know I'll get well."

"But the actual pain? Does it go?"

"It's difficult to tell. It seems to. But pain's a curious thing, isn't it? It can be there and you not notice it some-times. Other times there's nothing else."

"Not if it's severe. You must notice it then. How can you not?"

He spoke with the healthy man's unreasoned fear of unknown pain, and her eyes softened. "You'd be surprised. It's strange, but the pain can be there and not touch you, you seem to be outside, looking in."

He said huskily, "Is the pain often very bad?"

"Oh no. Most of the time I don't feel anything at all."

"How often is it—bad?"

"It varies so much. Days together there's nothing, then suddenly it comes. There seems to be no—no pattern. It must be something I do or don't do, I don't know what."

Just once—one night—he knew she was in pain. She lay rigidly beside him, her knees drawn up, catching her breath sharply like a sobbing child. Overcoming his own fear, in the darkness he began massaging her body and under his hand felt her womb knotted and hard, tensed against further pain. He did not know if it was the right thing to do, but he kept up his gentle movements and after a while, perhaps a quarter of an hour, he felt her go slack again and withdrew his hand.

"Was it very bad that time?"

"Yes. Like a spasm. It didn't last very long, though."

"Quite long enough."

She said, suddenly drowsy, "I'm sorry I woke you. I didn't mean to."

"It doesn't matter. Now go to sleep." He lay awake while she slept, filled with an anguished tenderness for his wife.

His love for her, indeed, had become deeper than ever before—either that, or he had just realized how much she meant to him. Yet for the first time in all the years of their marriage he began regularly visiting the tarts' quarter. It was somehow outside his marriage—a mechanical expedient like bloodletting to relieve a physical tumescence, in no way related to the feelings he bore for his wife, and in no sense putting them in jeopardy.

Even here there were involutions. That first assignation with a whore, after he had first learned what was wrong with Sarojini, still tore at his guts, bathing him in a bitter sweat and keeping him awake at night. That had been wrong, a sin, a betrayal. Yet now he could walk through those notorious streets where at upper windows you could glimpse the waiting women with their painted eyes and their hennaed nails, make his choice, think nothing of it, sleep the sounder. Worries, inevitably, came with it. It was expensive. It was not safe, and he knew himself to be too much of a novice to make it so. It upset his daily routine, and this detail proved the worst irritant of all. He had hardly realized before the extent to which he derived his well-being from the regular evening meal, surrounded by his family, at the end of the day's work. Now, by the time he had straggled home after one of his couplings, the girls had usually finished and gone, and Sarojini waited with lowered eyes and in silence. Or sometimes—increasingly, she was turning more and more to the Swami—she was not there at all, and in the bleak kitchen he would find cold curd-rice, a glutinous ooze from standing wrapped in a greasy banana leaf. I cannot stand it, he thought, eating the grayish mulch, surveying the unmade beds, noticing the unswept floor. I cannot. Yet he did not see what else he could do. An acceptant endurance was however beyond him; he suffered while he endured, unable either to overlook or to accept his changed condition.

More and more frequently he began to wonder—forlornly, passionately—why all this had had to happen. It almost rent him, the unnecessary quality of what was happening, big and small, to distort his life. It took him some time even to acknowledge that his *why* might be a universal cry, that a great many people as blameless as he were being gouged from grooves they had made for themselves and exposed dangling like blindworms to airs and blights whose existence they had not suspected.

Despite their respective preoccupations the protection of their children still exercised Dandekar and his wife. Sarojini worked strenuously and slept as little as she could to make up for the time she spent away. To account for these absences they jointly concocted tangled stories which subsequently tripped them up—a performance watched with puzzled interest by their curious daughters.

"I've told you. I go to see my friend. She's all alone."

"If she's all alone, why doesn't she come and live here?" This was Ramabai, the more persistent of the two.

"There's no room. Where would she sleep?"

"In the courtyard. Granny used to. And when we lived upstairs I remember she used to sleep in the kitchen."

"Your granny was used to it. Besides, she was our flesh and blood, we had to take her in."

"Why don't her relatives do the same for her?"

"I've just told you, she's quite alone."

"Then who looks after her when you're not there?"

"I suppose the neighbors help."

"Then why do you have to too?"

"Because she's a very old friend of mine. Because one must always do as much as one can."

"If she's an old friend why don't we know her?"

"She's only just come to live in this town."

"But you've never lived anywhere else, have you? You and Father?"

"I did as—as a child."

"Where?"

"Now, Ramabai!" Dandekar tried to be light but firm. "It's time you did some homework. Really, I've never known anyone except a lawyer ask so many questions."

"I only asked. I only wanted to know."

"Go along now."

Afterwards, worn out, he said, "Why don't you tell her and be done with it?"

"Tell her what?" Sarojini was equally tired.

"Where you go and why. Tell her what's wrong with you."

"No!" Sarojini answered vehemently. "It's not something you tell a girl of her age. My mother told me when I was twelve. I don't want her to be frightened as I was."

Dandekar was silent. Ramabai was twelve, verging on puberty. It did not make matters easier.

Ramabai became his next concern. He came home one night, late, to find Lakshmi alone. The maid had gone. With the erratic hours they kept she could hardly be blamed, and indeed nowadays she went when she thought fit. Fortunately for them, she was a conscientious girl. He said, frowning, "Where is your sister?"

Lakshmi was doing her sums. She said, frowning also, "Gone to the milk bar."

"Milk bar? Which one?" His stomach turned over. These days, he knew, girls and young men went to milk bars, and he also knew from hearsay what a very mixed lot was to be found there. He often said he realized times were changing, yet he had never thought his own daughter would gravitate to one of these places.

"The usual one—in Mahatma Gandhi Road. She was feeling hungry."

"Why? Didn't she eat her dinner?"

"There wasn't any to eat."

My God, he thought, how direct children are—forthright, uncompromising in their innocence. He said gently, "And you? Aren't you hungry?"

"I was. It's worn off now. Besides, I've eaten some copra. I found it in the store cupboard."

"That's not enough. I'll see if I can get you something more."

He went uncertainly into the kitchen. In all his life he had never cooked a meal, never fried a chili or a potato. Men never did, unless they were cooks, and even cooks wouldn't cook in their own homes. He poked around and found some pappadams in a tin but could not find the oil in which to fry them. There was a jar of mango pickle, curds in a pot, a little stale sliced bread. He took these in, but the child, used to rice, pulled a face at the bread. Then, hot and flustered, Sarojini came in. She had been held up—the widow she looked after had been taken worse—she made up some incoherent story for Lakshmi's benefit as she prepared a hurried meal.

Dandekar left them, went out of the house and down to Mahatma Gandhi Road where the milk bar was. It was no more than a long, narrow room with a marble-topped counter that ran the length of it and a crush of stools in front and two or three jumbled rows behind. All he could see from the outside was a tangle of legs twined about the chromium, in which he could not distinguish Ramabai's. The wooden half doors swung too quickly to allow him a proper look. He debated whether to go in and fetch her, disliking the idea; but in a few minutes she came out, followed by a girl he vaguely placed as a school friend called Lalita. Behind, shepherding the girls, came a youth of sixteen or seventeen whom he did not know.

"Ramabai." Dandekar spoke sharply as they came abreast of him. "Say good night to your friends. Your mother is waiting for you."

The girl obeyed; probably she had been on the point of doing so herself, but her face grew sulky.

"Who was your friend?" He tried to tone his voice down.

"Lalita."

"The other one?"

"Gopal."

"I don't think I know him," said Dandekar. "And you know we've told you you should never go out with people whom your mother and I don't know."

"Why not?" Half-child, half-woman, she whirled to face him. "Doesn't Mother go to see someone none of us know? Don't you?"

What does she know, what *does* she know? he thought, staring into those stormy eyes. Then he realized she was not an adult, that she was simply stating what she knew to be so, there was no treacherous innuendo.

"Yes of course we do, sometimes," he said, "but we're older, we have more experience, we know how to judge people. . . ."

He was on familiar ground, he had often spoken to his daughters on these lines and believed in what he said, yet now he felt strangely uncertain. His uncertainty made him angry, he labored his words and his voice grew domineering. When he had finished he felt no better. He stole a glance at his daughter; her face was rebellious and her mouth was sour. They finished the walk in silence.

Later he said to Sarojini, "Do you know why Ramabai was so late tonight?"

"Oh, I expect she stayed talking with one of her school friends." Sarojini, who had been sitting quite still, began to put her workbox in order.

"No. She went to a milk bar. Did you know she often went there?"

"She may have mentioned it." She avoided his eye.

He said heavily, "I don't think it's very desirable, do you? A girl of her age?"

"It isn't." She looked directly at him. "If I were here— or if you were—when she came home, perhaps she wouldn't. She never used to. But you know I have to go, and you know where I go."

"I know, I know," he said hurriedly. He had been convinced the fault was Sarojini's, it simply had not occurred to him that it might also be his; and the sudden imbalance produced by her words left him in confusion. "I'm not blaming you . . . I must try and get home more early, but lately we have been extraordinarily busy and—"

She accepted his story, her eyes once more lowered, and he was left to conjecture what lay behind those lids, how much she knew.

That night he kept himself and Sarojini awake with an uncontrollable restlessness, and when at last he slept, Sarojini's voice woke him, saying distinctly although she was fast asleep, "If Ramabai loses her good name she'll never marry well." But guilt over their daughter, though obviously shared, did not become any lighter.

# 16

THE third month was ending—the third month of a new epoch from which he now dated his life. The girls, twice disappointed, would not be expecting new-month presents, but he felt strongly the need for some sign of *rapprochement*, some visible token that would tell his daughters—especially Ramabai—that he was sorry for his ill-humors. In point of fact he was by no means certain that they did notice; but either way, he felt, it would do no harm to give them an occasional treat. The idea was still germinating when, with that curious communication of many years' marriage, Sarojini voiced it.

"I was wondering if you could get the girls something this month. . . . I know they miss it."

"I was thinking the same thing."

Their eyes met and Sarojini smiled slightly; this had

happened before. For a moment or two there was a flicker, a sense of their old companionship.

"Anything will do . . . quite small . . . and don't worry about me. But only if you have time of course." Her lids came down again.

"I'll make time," he answered, not looking at her.

They were fleeing each other again.

He had had some inkling all along; when he took stock he knew he had not the money. They could live reasonably on his hundred and twenty rupees a month; but for the last three months there had been no reason whatever in their ways. Oversleeping from uneasy nights, three days out of six Dandekar found it imperative, to get to work in time, to travel by bus. There had been the docking of two day's pay by Ghose, plus a ten-rupee fine. In that month he had left the rent unpaid, on which the formidable interest charged by his landlord was accumulating. There were prostitutes' costs; and, he now recalled, the spool of memory remorselessly unwinding, the money he had given in so cavalier a fashion to beggars, the boatman, the Swami, to Cousin Rajam, the unnecessary purchase of an expensive umbrella—the list seemed endless. Sarojini had not helped; on four occasions recently she had asked for extra housekeeping money, throwing responsibility onto a vague money-goes-nowhere-today.

He met these demands by getting salary advances (each time sanctioned by Chari), but he gave her the money grudgingly, knowing that the neglect of her duties—entrusting a servant girl with the shopping, the buying of pickles and relishes which were once her function, the purchase of shop clothes for the children which she had once made herself—was as much to blame as a rise in the cost of living.

Now he had not even the few rupees he needed, and the thought appalled him.

With a sinking heart he sat down to consider ways and means—he had made a promise, and he was a man of his word. An appeal for another advance he ruled out at once. Chari had made it clear he did not like his clerks overspending; and Dandekar himself felt in his bones that only the reckless, the irresponsible, and servants existed perpetually a month in advance. He might ask Sastri for a small loan; but again his instincts ran counter to this—the instincts of a man who has never known either riches or poverty, and so has never learned to be casual over money of whatever derivation. He considered deducting what he wanted from the household—water or electricity. But what is the good? he thought hopelessly. They only mount up, and in the end have to be met and it is ten times worse.

He left his easy chair and began pacing the courtyard

162

up and down in front of the tulasi tree. Presently he stopped. "If you were God," he said to the dark-leaved tree, "you would tell me what to do, show me the way—some reasonable way out." He stared almost hypnotically at the tree, willing it with a half-fearful temerity to make some sign; and then his eyes fell on the four silver lampions, one at each corner of the brass. He stooped and picked one up, weighing it in his hand. The silver alone would be worth four or five rupees, not counting the silversmith's labor . . . two of them would solve his problem. He picked up another lampion, clasping the two in both hands against his chest, gazing at the tree with exultation, with awe, with a sudden fear that came from nowhere and drew his scalp tight. "I cannot take what belongs to tulasi, to God," he whispered, and heard the silver clatter to the floor. He stared at them stupidly; one of the holders was dented, oil was dripping from the other. He bent and righted them, and felt his fright replaced by anger. "*You* made me think of taking them," he raged at the impersonal tree. "I would never have thought of it, never, you put it into my head and then you made me think it was wrong—just like the god that you must be, no one else could be capable of such a thing, such duplicity, not even a—"

"Father!" Lakshmi, wide-eyed, burst in. "What was that noise? It sounded like thieves."

"Thieves don't make such a noise." He pulled himself together. "It was me, I tripped over one of those—no, no, I'll clear it up, you go back and play."

But already she was kneeling, spooning up the spilled oil, putting the lampions back in their corners. "The tulasi," she breathed, and reverently touched her closed eyelids before the tree in apology for him.

When she had gone he did the same, touching each eyelid delicately with the tips of his fingers. "The tree is not God," he whispered, "but it is a symbol of God." With shaking hands he trimmed the wicks and lit the tiny flames.

He knew he would never again touch the vessels of God, but in the locked trunk lay a silver ashtray that would do equally well. It was shaped like a water lily, and had been given to him long ago by Wilson, his English boss, who did not like ashtrays shaped like water lilies. Only Englishmen could afford expensive dislikes like that. Dandekar did not like the idea of parting with it (he had been fond of Wilson), but he was in no position to afford expensive fads. He would have to sell it, and the heavy, solid silver would fetch enough to solve more than his present difficulties.

First, however, there was the locked trunk. Sarojini would give him the key, but would want to know what he sought, and somehow he shrank from telling her, the long train of cause and effect it would entail. I'll just say books, he thought. She doesn't know much about them, or if she asks I'll make up some story. . . . He assured himself it would be easy, but it was a relief nevertheless when he got hold of the keys without having to ask. They were lying conspicuously on the bed where anyone coming into the room, he thought disapprovingly despite his relief, could hardly have failed to notice them. He picked them up, looking around to make sure he was alone, then quickly, with guilt enveloping him like a mantle, he stooped and pulled the trunk out from under the bed.

The floor was gritty with dust. The trunk came out with a strident screech that set his teeth on edge. He waited, listening, but the girls were up on the terrace, Sarojini was not back, and the maid—well, he was master of this household, entitled to take what he chose. Still he hesitated, the keys in his hand, looking down at the box. He had opened it once, and his peace had splintered. Was he to open it again and pulverize the pieces that remained? He shook himself angrily. I'm becoming a foolish, superstitious old woman, he said to himself, and flung open the box.

It looked exactly the same, at first. Neatly packed and arranged, and an aroma of camphor and sandal from the layers of tissue and mull. His fears evaporated. He squatted down and began unpacking the trunk, mistily remembering that the ashtray was somewhere near the bottom. Sarojini's saris, the gold tissue, the small inherited pieces of jewelry—these he lifted carefully out and laid on the floor. The next layer was the silver—he could tell from the linen wrappings, but he could not decide which of the swathed shapes concealed his water lily.

With more haste now he began unwinding the linen, looping the coils about his wrist until he came to the stone. He gaped at it stupidly, he could not make anything of it at all—that lump of rock where silver should be, wrapped as if it were gold. When realization came he knew what more he would find, and methodically he began unwrapping what remained, carefully resetting the stones that emerged each in its broken cocoon. Then, defeated, he sank down on his haunches, surrounded by ruin.

"What are you doing?"

He turned, ashen-faced, and she was ashen too. He got to his feet and dusted himself, stepped carefully over the debris and sat down on the bed.

"I was looking for the Englishman's ashtray," he said simply. "It's not there. Do you know where it is?"

She was still standing in the doorway, framed by it, rigid.

"Yes." Her voice had no body, it was like dead leaves. "I have given it away."

"The other silver?"

"That too."

He could only look at her; there was nothing to say. If she hadn't given away their silver he would have sold it—dispersed their joint holding, the hoard inherited and accumulated and meant in time for their children, as she had done. The knowledge killed his anger. We are being driven, he thought. We are straddling a tiger that we cannot dismount.

She said, tonelessly, "I'm sorry. I had to."

"Whom did you give it to?" He knew, but he had to ask. Where else should it go but into that insatiable maw that had opened in front of them, exacting its dues with an impersonal compulsion which no one could pin down, none in their senses credit?

She had made no answer, and he said, "The Swami. That's where it went, didn't it?"

"No. Not to him personally. He has no use for money."

"Just generally then."

She nodded silently. She's frightened, he thought, but he could not bring himself to say that it did not matter. He squatted down once more and slowly repacked the trunk. When he had finished he locked it, took the key off the ring and handed back the bunch to her.

"Perhaps it's safer with me," he said, trying not to sound too bitter, trying indeed to smile; but then he thought, appalled, Perhaps it's no safer with me, and the corners of his mouth grew as pinched and white as hers.

The trunk stayed locked, but he sold his watch. The proceeds made possible the usual end-of-the-month presents for the children, although for the life of him he could not go through the charade of getting something for Sarojini. It also made possible a modest Deepavali—a festival for which he would normally have put by a reasonable sum, but which this year was upon him almost before he was aware of it. Well, his watch—it had been a good one—would pay for that too: for Deepavali, festival of lights, of feasting, of gaiety, the cheer of giving and receiving. He sighed as, together, they made their purchases. A skirt for Lakshmi—tangerine silk with a mango border. A coin-patterned green silk for Ramabai. A cotton shirt for the boy. Jacket cloth for the maid. Exotic ingredients for the special festival dishes, expensive even though pared to the minimum.

Nobody would guess we were anything but well off, Dandekar thought, grimly surveying the handsome spread, the girls glowing in their bright new clothes; but soon the festival got the better of him and he thought, almost cheerfully, We're not all that badly off—a little retrenchment here and there, no luxuries and we'll yet replace our silver. He beamed at his family, went peacefully to bed, and was at his desk in the morning with time to spare, having walked all the way.

Possibly he knew even then he was pulling alone, but had succeeded in shutting it out of his mind. A few weeks later, however, the door swung violently open with the discovery that Sarojini had taken the thin gold chain that adorned the baby's neck. Adversity had sharpened his senses—ordinarily he would never have noticed it was missing. When he did, what he remembered was the year's hard saving that had gone into its purchase, this birthday present for their only son, and his voice was sharp as he questioned the maid.

"Where is the chain?" He eyed her suspiciously.

"Chandru-baba's?" The girl shifted the child on her hip, returning his gaze with indignation. "Mistress took it from him herself. For repolishing, she said, though it looked shiny enough to me. She said yourself would be taking it to the goldsmith to have it done."

"Yes, that's right. To the goldsmith," he muttered. "I— quite forgot."

He knew it wasn't convincing, but he was too tired to fabricate, to put some substance in the flimsy story. And anyway, he thought, she must realize by now something's going on, she'd be a half-wit if she didn't. He glanced guardedly at the girl, and was immediately irritated by the conspiratorial look she returned.

*169*

"It's two weeks gone," she volunteered. "Since the mistress took it."

"I know," he said shortly. "Get on with your work, will you? There's enough left undone."

He left them and went into the bedroom. Outside he could hear the maid banging about and grumbling audibly, and Chandru, who had caught her mood, whimpering. It's the small things that break you, he said to himself, nerves on edge from the noise, but when he began thinking of bigger things some kind of insulation encased him, he no longer heard either the servant or his son.

# 17

HE had not even formulated what he would say. All he knew was that he must go to the Swami—words would come later—and blindly he made his way to the whitewashed house with the anguished prayer that the Swami would be there and not in his village fastness.

He had been twice before, and on both occasions the doors had stood open. Now a low wooden palisade barred the entrance. He could have scaled it easily enough, but the privacy of property was well ground into him. After some hesitation he rattled the barrier, at first gently but soon with vigor. In crises the office tended to recede, but this time he had managed to anchor it in the middle distance where it still mattered, and if it could possibly be done he intended to get to it on time.

"What is it? Are you on fire?" The disagreeable voice seemed to rise from the ground, and peering through the bars Dandekar saw the dwarf lying like a watchdog at the entrance, swathed in a heavy shawl against the morning dew.

"I came to see the Swami," Dandekar said, feeling oddly guilty. "Is he not awake?"

"What do you think, at this time?"

"It's seven o'clock. After seven, I'd say."

"Depends when you sleep when you wake. Last night it was four o'clock before we lay down. One of your sort he was—came here sniveling, wanting to see the Swami and making more noise than you are. Then he wouldn't go away. Four o'clock. Now you're here, I suppose I better get up."

"I'm sorry," Dandekar stammered. "I didn't know—"

"As well get up now as try to sleep." The dwarf yawned, kicked aside the shawl and stood up. He was quite naked. Despite himself Dandekar could not keep his eyes from that disturbing, squatly telescoped body. The dwarf himself seemed not to care. Grunting with cold he rooted among the gunny sacks on which he had been lying for his clothes, finally pulling out a crumpled dhoti, a child's-size shirt.

"What do you want with the Swami?"

Dandekar started; his thoughts had wandered. "I wanted to—to ask him something."

"What?"

"A favor."

"What sort?"

"I'd prefer to—to tell him," said Dandekar painfully. "It's—personal."

"That's what they all say. Come along then, I'll take you to him. No one turned away, that's his rule even if it kills him."

The dwarf led the way through the courtyard where Dandekar had seen the congregation in prayer, up a flight of stairs and to a veranda on the upper floor.

"There he is." He pointed. "Don't stay long, he's tired."

Dandekar did not immediately see the Swami. It was a long, narrow veranda with a towering balustrade well over his height, and light seemed to bounce disturbingly between the polished black of the cuddapah stone floor and the dead white of the balusters, making perception difficult. Then in one of the interstices—almost at his feet, so that he started—merged in shadow, his face nearly as white as one of the columns against which he leaned, Dandekar saw the Swami.

"Are you in trouble?" It was the same question, gently asked and easy enough to answer, yet as before Dandekar had no words.

"There's no hurry. It will come when you are ready." The Swami was not looking at him, he did not seem to have to look at anything, to do anything, he was simply there. Dandekar sat down, glancing covertly at the thin face, the weatherworn skin, the calm, deep-set eyes. After a while he forgot even those externals, aware only of a quiet that seeped into him, a stillness in which he seemed to float, detached from every care, warm and serene like a child in the womb.

"Is it Sarojini?" The cord was cut, not ruthlessly but with definition.

"Yes." Dandekar roused himself. "She has taken—given away—a gold chain without my knowledge."

No sooner had he said it than it seemed puerile, extraordinary only in that it should exercise a grown man.

"It's not only that." He hurried on. "She has taken other things—things that were meant for our children, silver, jewelry—two pieces, which was all we possessed—any number of things. . . ."

"Your possessions matter a great deal to you?" The Swami spoke quietly, his eyes seemed to darken and grieve for him, for humanity, and Dandekar longed to say, passionately: "No, they don't matter a pin's head." But truth drew him back.

"No," he said hoarsely, forcing himself to the shameful admission. "They don't matter at all now, when I am sitting here with you. But they will, later, and that later is reality to me, in which I must live." He paused, licking his dry lips. "You see, we are not rich people, we cannot afford to give away so much."

The Swami did not answer, but in the silence Dandekar

knew what he was thinking, resisted the knowledge until it bore him down and the words burst from him.

"One is not rich until one has nothing left to give away," he said, clenching his hands. "I know it, I know it's true, but I can't do it, it's asking too much of me, from ordinary people like me, I—"

"I know." The Swami's low voice halted his frenzy. "I do not ask."

"But you take," cried Dandekar. "Sarojini gives and gives and you do not stop her."

"If I were to compel her not to give, I would also be free to compel her to give. That is the other face of the coin, the other half of what you ask. Can you not see it?"

"Even so I want her to stop," Dandekar cried stubbornly, childishly. "I want you to make her stop."

"Compulsion is the beginning of corruption." The Swami looked at him steadily, holding him so that there was no escape. "It is an eating away of the spirit of whoever does it, and whoever has it done to him. Is that what you want?"

Neither spoke again, and in the long quiet for the first time since their original encounter Dandekar saw the Swami as a man. He was sitting as he had been, resting against a pillar, his hands unmoving in his lap; but now his eyes were closed, his head thrown back in exhaustion, and the light fell full on a face lit by pallor and creased with fatigue—creases that might go with rest in another, but in this man were already hardened into lines. He gives too much of himself, Dandekar thought, gives and gives—am I mad, taxing him with taking?

He stayed for a while longer, half lost in the peace that, still, he felt in the Swami's presence; then at last he rose and went softly down the stairs.

"Thought you had taken root up there." The surly whisper rose from the stair well and the dwarf came out. "Thought I told you not to stay too long, too."

"I'm sorry," said Dandekar. "I lost count of time."

"Take and take," said the dwarf. "Then come here bleating about what you give—what your wife gives rather, a mouse couldn't feed off what you've brought— as if there was nothing in the world bar money."

Dandekar stood still. "You listened," he said. "You heard every word."

"Of course I did. I hear everything that goes on around here."

"Is that what you're here for?"

"Among other things." The yellowish eyes in the pug face narrowed. "If you mean am I kept and paid for that— Is that what you mean?"

"Are you?"

"Kept? Paid? No. I've sold myself before—people paid to see me and then they saw less than you did." The dwarf stopped and eyed Dandekar contemptuously. "You still want to know why I'm here? Because I don't want my spirit all squashed and twisted like the body you couldn't take your eyes from, that's why."

"I didn't mean—" began Dandekar, shocked.

"I don't mind," said the dwarf. "I just notice. I used to notice in the old days too, outside"—he gestured toward the street—"and I used to pray to God and the devil that they would be blinded, never see again . . . but it's no good to you that sort of heat—it melts you up, leaves a shapeless mess inside instead of what was meant to be. I've never sizzled like that since I've been here and I'm thankful for that and I stay and do what I can to save him from people like you."

"People like me? I haven't—"

"Yes, people like you. Misers, clinging to your gold chains and your silver cups, grudging every anna—"

It's not true, Dandekar thought, looking at the upturned accusing face, checking the hot rejoinder. We're not rich, we never have been, we never will be.

"—that your wife has brought. How do you think we care for everyone who comes here? No one is turned away—no one, do you hear? And *I'm* the one who sees to it that they're fed and clothed and mended, patched up into human beings again—I, I, I! See there?" He took hold of Dandekar's jacket, dragged him into the courtyard, past the startled crowd now assembled there, beyond into the storerooms where the sacks of grain stood, the teak chests filled with rice that Dandekar had seen before, the tall jars of oil. "They've all got to be filled." The dwarf's face was mottled, marbled yellow in his passion. "And kept filled. It isn't done by sorcery. Nor by force. Nor by letting people grab what they want and grudge any return."

"I didn't know," said Dandekar gently. "I didn't realize."

There was a five-rupee note in his pocket. He handed it to the dwarf and went out.

It was ten o'clock. An indifferent clock somewhere tolled out the time. The office, Chari, Ghose, grew life-large and threatening again. He had re-entered his world of reality.

# 18

DANDEKAR knew, how, what Sarojini had meant. When you were with the Swami, actually there, nothing material, or physical, mattered. You saw them for the worthless trumperies that they were, rose above your body, knew for a while the meaning of peace. Then you came away and the pains crept back, the worry, the misery, the lust for gold chains and silver cups.

It's all very well, he reflected a few days later, well and good for those who can, but who will replenish *my* chests and coffers? And I have a sick wife, and two daughters whose dowries I have yet to provide, and a son to be settled in life. . . . They danced across his ledgers, his wife, his daughters, his responsibilities, and he thought, desperately trying to put sense into the figures before him, I must try again to get Sarojini away from him, because our worlds do not mix. It is disastrous to try to make them.

It was a forlorn hope; he seized it because it was the only one. He sought out Sarojini's Cousin Rajam.

Rajam and Sarojini had, until lately, been quite close. It had often puzzled him that the loud, rollicking Rajam and his grave, quiet-spoken wife should get along at all, let alone so well together. It had, indeed, often irritated him; but now, anxiously, he wondered if he could ask her —relying on their friendship—to wean Sarojini away from the Swami, get her to see it was no good, no earthly use. Perhaps if he put himself in Rajam's hands, explained everything, he might persuade her to persuade Sarojini— the words were all twisted and tangled, he decided to leave it to the actual meeting to sort out.

Rajam gave him her usual robust welcome, and indeed, swamped by her effervescence, it was some time before Dandekar could make himself heard. A little to his relief Rajam seemed to know all about Sarojini and the Swami, although apparently Sarojini had not seen fit to confide in her.

"Perhaps she had her reasons," said Rajam heavily, without belief. "I must say I was astonished when I heard. I should have thought I'd be the first person she'd tell, wouldn't you? After all we're cousins! And—"

"How did you hear?"

"Oh, things get around, you know," said Rajam vaguely. "And if it's anything to do with the Swami, well, everyone knows him, except of course people like you."

"What do you mean, people like me?"

"No offense meant, Cousin. I only meant people like—well, you know, you've worked for, been trained by the British, you don't believe in anything much, do you? That's all I meant."

"The British have been gone ten years," said Dandekar with asperity. "Which of their brands does my forehead still bear? What beliefs do I lack?"

"Well, the Swami . . ." Rajam's eyes grew round in her chubby face. "He is a good man, Cousin, and he has powers . . . you must believe in them, even if things don't always go your way."

"Do they ever go one's way?" cried Dandekar. "Sarojini has relied on his powers for several months now. Is she cured? She doesn't know, I don't know—but if she were, why is she still going to him day after day? She says she feels better when she's there, when she comes back, even I know he gives you some strange sort of peace, but is there anything else to it? Is there *ever* anything else?"

"Don't say such things, Cousin." Rajam pursed her lips disapprovingly. "You are belittling what you don't know. It must be your contact with Europeans—even if it was ten years ago—that makes you so rash."

"And what makes you so gullible," cried Dandekar, "as to believe these miraculous tales, these hearsay stories, these cures that have happened always to someone else?"

"He cured me," said Rajam simply.

Dandekar almost gasped. Here, at last, was what he had been seeking—the evidence that someone had been healed, and if so that Sarojini might be, and then what did a gold chain matter, what did anything matter as long as she was well? He said, eagerly discarding all his previous plans, "Did he really cure you? You're quite sure?"

"Of course I'm sure," said Rajam indignantly. "I used to get such terrible pains—here—almost doubled me up they did, but the doctors couldn't do anything for me. In fact do you know what they said? That I was imagining then! As if anyone could imagine pain like that, and me of all people! And as if one would want to!"

"But was there anything wrong? Actually, physically wrong?"

"I've just told you—they said not. What they meant was *they* couldn't find anything wrong. But I can tell you, Cousin, I would have died if the pain had gone on. Luckily I went to the Swami . . . and I've never had it even once since, may God bless him. Why, Cousin, you're not going already?"

"I may as well," said Dandekar wearily. "I came to—well, it doesn't matter now."

He had known all along it was a forlorn hope, but with it gone—Rajam entrenched in her beliefs, the firm evidence of a cure as elusive as before—he faced despair. I'm in the grip of something which I cannot control, he said to himself, walking slowly away from the mean little street where Rajam lived. The best—the only—thing I can do is live from day to day and see what each one brings. Only fools fight. The idea chilled him, it was a coldness closing around his heart. What I need is a little warmth, he thought, frightened, and at once there came to mind the pleasures he had eschewed, the women who would serve him, give him a brief release. He would be anguished afterwards, he knew, but one must live in the present and now was not afterwards. He changed direction and began to walk faster.

Even that hope, however, turned to ashes. The woman was well-meaning, conscientious, determined to give value for his money. Conditioned by his own marriage, Dandekar wanted from her nothing beyond a passive acquiescence. He was too shy to tell her so. With something near to embarrassment he bore her energetic movements, her simulated sounds of passion, her artificial frenzy, and found his own vigor flagging.

"What's the matter?"

"Nothing."

"If you don't want to why did you come?"

"I'm sorry," he said. "I've been doing too much lately. I didn't realize it."

"Oh, that's why . . . so long as I was all right."

"You were all right." He felt wretched. He got up to go, paid the woman, and then he noticed the carved blackstone group on the cluttered ledge above the cot and was instantly afire again. He stood rigidly, unable to take his eyes from the nude interlocked limbs, rubbed shiny with and exuding rancid oil, and from a distance heard the woman say, hinting exasperation, "If you wanted help why couldn't you say so? I could have shown you pictures better than that. You can't come back now, not for the same price. Fair's fair."

He jerked himself into motion, and without a word hurried out into the street and began walking away from the house; but he had not gone far when he stopped and felt in his pockets. Then, heavy with self-reproach, he turned and retraced his steps.

It was dark when he got out again. The solitary lanterns gave out a feeble yellow light that expired long before the next lamppost loomed, leaving great dipping pools of uneven blackness between. Nearer home it was better. The gas lamps, newly lit, flared brightly, dispersing the night in a greenish brilliance. From the street the tenement looked almost pleasant, with that pale sheen hiding its peeling imperfections, and lights twinkling genially from the serried stories.

His own part of the house was in darkness. It must be another of Sarojini's evenings out, he thought, or else she and the children were unwontedly early in bed. He went cautiously into his room and after listening for a few moments to make sure Sarojini was not asleep there he switched on the light. If Sarojini was out one or both of the girls must be in, he thought, standing uncertainly in the empty room; they wouldn't go out leaving Chandru alone. Perhaps they were on the terrace; they sometimes went up there if it was stuffy, even when in charge of the child, though they never stayed away too long. He waited a little for them to come down, and when they didn't he decided they must be in their rooms, asleep, and he tiptoed in to make certain.

Both beds were empty; he could tell that even without the light, but he could also tell there was someone in the room. More puzzled than alarmed he reached for the switch, and as he did so Ramabai's voice, husky and strained, said, "Don't put on the light, Father. I've got a headache, it hurts my eyes."

It was too late, the light was on, and he saw Ramabai crouched beside her bed, her face blotchy and smudged with hastily wiped tears.

"What are you doing sitting all by yourself in the darkness?" he said sympathetically. "Where is Lakshmi?"

"She's playing outside. I told her to go—I didn't want to, with this headache."

"Then you should be in bed," he said kindly, going to her side. "Come along now, lie down and I'll find you some aspirin." He bent to take her arm, but to his surprise she shrank back.

"No! I don't want any aspirin. I just want to be left alone."

He thought she was being difficult—in one of her increasingly frequent moods that varied from pert to sulky. He said firmly, taking her arm, "Come on now. You can't sit there on the floor—"

"Don't touch me!"

His hand dropped with the sheer shock of it. He stared at his daughter's pinched face, understanding that this was not just a mood, but not knowing how to deal with the situation. He was no good with children—awkward even with his own daughters though he was extremely fond of them. For one piercing, shattering moment he wondered if she knew, forswearing in that split second all his peccadilloes if only she didn't; then he dismissed the thought. He had been careful; no one was likely to know, let alone pass it on to a child.

"Is the pain bad?" he said gently. "Just tell me if there's anything you want, then I'll go away and you can sleep."

"I want my mother." Her control gave way suddenly, she was gulping and gasping with the strength of her sobs.

"What is it, Rani pet?" he said, wrung. "You don't often cry like this. What has happened?"

"Nothing. Nothing at all."

He knelt beside her, meaning to draw her close, but again she shrank away. "You mustn't come near. You mustn't."

"All right, I won't." He moved away, and suddenly he knew why she wanted him to keep at a distance. It was customary; women kept apart until the third day—even nowadays, although most of them did away with the ritual cleansing unless it happened to be convenient. He gazed helplessly at his daughter's tear-soaked face. Her mother should be here, he thought. There's nothing I can do, it's not my place.

"Your mother won't be very long," he said at last, gently, "and I'm in the next room if you want me. Don't cry any more, will you, pet? You might wake the baby and what would I do if you were both crying?"

He had managed to make her smile, but his own heart was heavy. Only fools fight, he thought, brooding in his room, but all men are fools when it comes to their children.

# 19

INEVITABLY he woke late the next morning, with a thick head and red-rimmed eyes that watered and smarted. Sarojini was in only slightly better shape—she had not looked well for months now—and Ramabai's face was still flushed and puffy from crying. My God, he thought, dabbing at his eyes, shaving frantically in front of the chipped mirror clamped to the bedpost, how terrible we all look, how terrible *I* look. Everybody will notice when I go in. And I'm going to be late again. He tried to speed up his shaving and the razor slipped, cutting his lip. Despite his efforts, probably because of them, the bleeding went on for a full ten minutes—he timed it, in a red frenzy, by the alarm clock on the window ledge. There was no question, of course, of a meal, nor of walking. He drank his coffee and ran for a bus.

He had to run again at the other end, but he made it,

turning in at the office gates with a few minutes still in hand.

"Just in time, eh?" said Joseph, who followed him into the office. "Just as well too, if you ask me. Though I wouldn't recommend running in this heat."

"I didn't ask you," said Dandekar shortly. "And since you mention it, running doesn't recommend itself to me either."

"Then why do it?" Joseph raised bland eyebrows. "All you have to do is deprive yourself of that extra ten minutes snuggling up to your beloved in bed. Can't have sensuality and punctuality, you know. That's life for you— the delectable and the detestable indissolubly linked together. If you want one you have to put up with the other."

"Oh stop talking," snapped Dandekar. "Why don't you get yourself a wife and make her listen to all this?"

"Not me," said Joseph, and he danced a few steps, singing, "A bachelor boy am I," which was the theme song—a freely translated and judiciously altered version of the unacknowledged original—of the film he had seen last night.

"You're hardly a boy," said Dandekar ungraciously.

"And it's only a song," said Joseph tartly. "I didn't mean it to refer to myself literally and specifically, I just happen to be singing it. Any objections?"

"None. Though I have heard better songs."

"I didn't compose it."

"And finer voices."

"I'm told mine is a very passable tenor."

"You should get yourself a wife," Dandekar smiled bleakly, "as I said before. She'd soon put you wise."

"Not me," said Joseph again. "I've told you before, I'm all for the happy state. A mistress any time—she knows she hasn't got you, she'll put herself out for you, but a wife? Now you're a married man. When did your wife last take the trouble to please you?"

"That's none of your bloody business," said Dandekar furiously. "If you must know—"

"Shut up, you two."

"Heaven's sake, you'll have the officers in."

"Are you trying to get us all sacked?"

There were a dozen interruptions. They all knew vaguely that Dandekar's trouble was to do with his wife —even Joseph, who had not really meant to go so far— and were appalled by the sudden ugly turn to the hitherto aimless and irritable bickering. Dandekar opened his files, and Joseph, on the verge of apologizing, was dissuaded from it by the hard and unrelenting set of his jaw.

The significance of the sudden chorus of consternation had not been lost on Dandekar—not even in his fury; and, later, he sounded Sastri about it.

"Of course they know there's something wrong," said Sastri heartily enough, but with an undercurrent of uneasiness. "After all, my dear chap, you're not exactly bursting with happiness these days, are you? And your work's—" Gone to pot, he had been about to say, but stopped himself. "—got a little behind," he finished. "Naturally no one listens, but Ghose doesn't always keep his voice down, does he?"

"Everyone seems to know it's Sarojini." Dandekar did not care about Ghose. "How do they know? I don't carry it on my face, do I?"

"Oh well," said Sastri, with an imprecision to surpass Rajam's. "Stories get around, you know . . . people will talk, it's what they've got tongues for. And of course in any office there's always a lot of gossip."

"What sort?"

"Well, seeing you like that—a bit fed up—they make up things to fit."

"What sort of things?"

"Well, you know Joseph and his bed talk . . . it gives everyone ideas, they seem to think Sarojini's having—having an affair. Of course *you* know, and I know, that Hindu women of our class simply don't have love affairs."

"An affair." Dandekar looked up queerly at Sastri. "I wish they were right. I wish to God she was."

"Don't talk like that." Sastri was deeply disturbed.

"You don't realize what you are saying. Our whole society rests on the virtue of our women, they are the foundation. I don't think you understand—"

"I don't think you understand," said Dandekar, "what I'm up against. If it were a man I'd rejoice, do you know that? I'd give anything to find it was true. If you'd told me six months ago I would have said it wasn't possible, I'd have looked the way you're looking now . . . but the way things are I'm fighting something invisible, there's nothing flesh and blood to take hold of and crush . . . I don't even know what I'm fighting, I just keep telling myself I must." He paused and looked at Sastri's anxious face. "When I believed there was another man I thought it was unbearable. But nothing is, is it? You find that out the next step on, when it gets worse. Do you think there's any limit? Or can you just go on and on, always looking back at what you left as better?"

"I don't know what's come over you," said Sastri helplessly. "You've got so strange and queer lately. Now you're even beginning to talk like a guru, and it's talk I've never understood, I just don't like so many questions without answers. And if you'd told me six months ago you'd be halfway to a guru I wouldn't have believed it either."

"I almost wish I were"—Dandekar put his throbbing head in his hands—"then perhaps I wouldn't be so—so hurt, by some of the things that have happened. Not just

to me, you know, but the—the children. Last night, seeing Ramabai like that, I knew I couldn't go on letting
things drift."

"You haven't exactly been letting things drift."

"No. But I cannot afford even that much leeway."

"What are you going to do?"

"Questions, questions, questions." Dandekar's knuckles
dug into his forehead. "They crowd into my brain and it's
as you said, I don't know the answers. I suppose it's because I've never had to think much about anything until
now, but I don't seem able to think straight, do anything.
All I know is I can't go on like this."

"Look here," said Sastri urgently. "You must get some
help—no, no, not me, I know I talk big"—he colored
slightly—"but I don't always fool myself. I'm an ordinary
man, a clerk—all right, a senior clerk—but I've no power,
I'm no good to you. You need someone—someone powerful to help you. This thing's too big for you alone."

Dandekar took his hands away, staring at the other
mutely. He was a clerk too, and clerks did not know men
of power, it was not in their scheme of living. Except
Chari. The thought must have occurred to both of them
simultaneously, although, lacking the courage, it was not
Dandekar but Sastri who voiced it.

"Ask him now." Sastri could feel Dandekar shying
away from the task. "Straightaway. It'll make you feel
better."

"Not now. I'll ask him tomorrow. It's too—too late, almost closing time."

"You've got nearly twenty minutes."

"It's not enough," said Dandekar desperately, "there's such a lot to explain and I—I don't feel up to it."

"It won't be any easier for keeping."

"I know, I know," cried Dandekar. "I tell you I'll see him tomorrow, it's beyond me now. I feel as if my head's on fire."

There was a short pause, while Sastri considered whether or not to let the matter rest there.

"Better be going back," he said at last, hoping that the fading light in the dingy sanctum was at least partially responsible for his friend's haggard face. "They'll be wondering what's happened to us."

Dandekar nodded, and in silence both men went back to their desks, their neglected files in the general office. Officers and clerks had gone, the cawing of roosting crows in the tamarinds had stilled, before the day's stint was done and the men left for home.

# 20

THE younger girl, Lakshmi, sent to wake him the following morning, started back in alarm when she saw her father.

"What's the matter?" He raised heavy eyes to the round perturbed face, groaning at the thought of getting up. "Do I look so terrible?"

"Your—your face. It's gone all ugly."

"Well," he said crossly, heaving himself out of bed, "no one looks pretty first thing in the morning. I'll be all right when I've washed."

Mentally he added an aspirin to the wash, for his head was throbbing so viciously that he could hardly see. His towel hung from a nail in the wall; he reached for it, feeling distinctly dizzy, and propped himself against the bedpost to shave. The child had been right, he thought, focusing with difficulty on his image in the chipped glass. His face did look awful. One eye was heavy-lidded and swollen, and the area above it and well into his scalp felt tight and hot. He put the razor down, and trying to hold himself steady began gingerly to feel the affected area with the tips of his fingers. Then the pain struck him, a streak like lightning that tore through face and brain, wrenching every nerve in its path. When it was gone he could not believe it, it had been so intense. He stared at his reflection in astonishment, stiff with shock, the palms of his hands wet with sweat. The pain had been all on one side of his face, above the left eye to the roots of his hair; the flesh still quivered from the impact, though the pain had now completely gone.

"Father!" It was Lakshmi, sent to summon him again. "Mother says to tell you to hurry, or you'll be late."

"I'm coming." I must have imagined it, he said to himself. There's nothing to see, just a little redness—probably from sitting in a draft, nothing more. He eyed himself narrowly in the glass, half-challenging the pain to return if it were real, almost convinced that it couldn't be, when it hit him again.

He lay down this time, covering his eyes with his hands while the fiery lash fell across his face. It was gone again in a few seconds, and then, the sweat pouring from him, he called Sarojini.

"Probably just a touch of neuralgia. Here—take these, yes, all three since the pain's so bad. I'll get you a cold compress in a minute."

He swallowed the tablets and lay back, closing his eyes. Sarojini, he thought dizzily, had always been very competent about illness. She gave unfrightening names to pain, but never minimized it, never said you were making a fuss about nothing. Perhaps it's because she knows what it's like, he thought. But she had always been like that—even before. In the next room he could hear her directing the maid to the ice factory, giving the girl explicit instructions.

"Ask for a block, you understand. I don't want any ice chips, they melt too quickly. And make sure they pack it in plenty of sawdust, don't come back with a boxful of water."

He had not heard her so brisk, so like her old self, for a long time. Even illness has its compensations, he thought; and then the thought came, timid and hesitant, that if he were sick longer, more seriously, he might yet wean her away from the Swami. Then what? Then get her cured by modern means. But she won't let herself be until the Swami goes, he thought. I've been through all this before, round and round like a squirrel in a cage. He had only seen it once, a small crazed creature that frantically trod the bars of its cylindrical prison, setting it revolving faster and faster to the delight of the crowd. Bells on the cylinder tinkled; hot sun beat down on the gray stiff fur. Poor thing, he thought in a comprehension of horror after so many long years, poor thing.

The maid was back with the ice. Through another burst of pain he heard them pounding it in the kitchen. In a few moments Sarojini came in.

"Here you are." Crushed ice tied in a child's balloon, wrapped around with flannel. "Hold it against your face where the pain seems worst."

He did so, and some slight relief spread over his hot face.

"I don't think I can manage the office today," he said weakly, "I—"

"I wouldn't even think of it. Not until you're quite well again."

"I'd better send them a note straightaway."

"Yes." She had ready paper, pen, ink in Lakshmi's non-spill bottle. "The maid's just going out to do the shopping. She can call in at your office first."

Three days' grace were allowed by the rules; after that he would have to provide, at his own cost, a doctor's certificate. He worried about that, about the mounting arrears of work, at the same time trying to sleep. In between, quite arbitrarily, the pain assaulted him. He gave up at last and sat up. To his surprise Sarojini was sitting on the ground at the foot of the bed, steadily sewing.

"Oh there you are," he said unnecessarily.

"Yes. Did you want something?"

"No, no. I thought perhaps you might have gone out."

"I'm not going anywhere today."

He gloated; this was a triumph, however minor and passing, over the Swami. When the fierce feeling was gone, sponged away by pain, her presence still had the power to soothe him. I want her there always, he thought, half-dozing, keeping his closing eyes on the dark smooth head he could just glimpse at the foot of his bed. That's her place, and that's where I want her.

He thought he felt better that evening, and with Saro-jini on one side and the servant girl on the other he struggled out to his easy chair in the courtyard. Despite his aches he even managed to remember Ramabai.

"She's all right." Sarojini handed him the freshly made buttermilk he had asked for. "It's quite natural, you know."

"All the same she was very upset. I think being alone—"

"We all have to be alone, at times."

Her tone was not vehement, not even sharp, but the interruption was decisive. She's answering me, he thought miserably. I wanted her to say she would always be with us, and she has refused. Why do we have to talk this way? What we mean comes along like invisible writing, underneath what we actually say.

He said suddenly, jerking up in his chair, "Is it very hot tonight? Or do you think I've got a fever?"

"It is hot." She rose with a rustle of her sari and felt his forehead. "No, I don't think you're running a temperature. Not more than half a degree at the most."

He fell back reassured. They had never replaced the inherited thermometer that Ramabai had broken at the age of three, relying instead on Sarojini's hand. It had been a trustworthy guide.

"Perhaps I'll be able to go back to the office tomorrow after all," he said hopefully. "If there's no fever there can't be anything much wrong, can there?"

But in the morning when he opened his eyes he forgot what he had said, he could only think about how ill he felt. The light was hurting his eyes. He turned his back on it, but even so it was too strong. Sarojini, who had spent the night on the floor, was busy in the kitchen, and rather than trouble her he got out of bed, cursing, to let down the blind in front of the window. Twin ropes held up the blind which, unfastened, should have let it unroll smoothly, shutting out the sun. Instead it descended in jerks and halfway down it stuck, leaving him with one rope slack and the other taut. He tugged at both savagely and the whole structure fell in a spray of plaster.

"Oh sir." The servant girl inopportunely arrived, was staring at him, the rubble around him.

"Don't stand there." He put his hand up to his eyes, blinded by the light. "Get a broom and sweep it up and go. Heaven's sake, what is there to gape at?"

"Oh sir, your face. It's come up red like pomegranate seed. Like the pox it is, sir. Oh sir."

They both knew about smallpox and looked at each

other aghast; then they were master and servant again and abruptly he dismissed her. Shakily he took down the glass and saw that the girl had been right; forehead and scalp were covered with blisters, some clear, some filled with blood-streaked fluid that looked like pomegranate seed. He was really frightened now; like the other government employees he had been vaccinated against smallpox, but this could be nothing else. Hoarsely he called Sarojini; then remembering, he halted her at the door.

"Don't come too near. You'll have to send for a doctor. It's smallpox."

"Smallpox?" Even now she was not flustered. "Let me see."

She was at his side. Making no more protest he turned full face to the window, where the strong white light of high summer beat in.

"It's not smallpox. You see it's all on one side, above the eye."

"Are you quite sure?" He was sweating.

"Quite sure," she said gently. "It's just some kind of unusual rash. You're not to worry now—I've sent for the doctor already. He ought to be here quite soon."

The doctor came late in the afternoon. It was his third visit to the family in ten years, and he knew he had only been called in because the patient had not been able to totter as far as the government hospital where payment in this income bracket was nominal. He was quite used to this; doctors' visits were a fearful luxury to most of the families he attended.

He was not a fashionable doctor. Without much difficulty he diagnosed the trouble.

"Shingles," he said cheerfuly. "Discomfort, yes, but nothing to worry about. It'll clear up in a week or two. Meanwhile make sure you use the eye drops, three times a day, and—"

"The children." Dandekar rose hazily from the sea of instructions and prescriptions. "Will they get it from me? Should they be kept—?"

"No, no. Nothing like that. It's not catching."

"Where did I get it from, then?"

"My dear man, a lot of people get diseases no one can tell where from!"

"There must be some cause," said Dandekar stubbornly. "Here I am come up in what looks like the pox— Is it a germ? Something I've eaten? There must be a cause."

"Well there isn't," said the doctor. "Or if there is we don't know it. Or if you want a good guess for your money I'd say you've been worrying a lot and your body's fed up with you and is showing it." And he departed, thoughtfully slipping his bill into Sarojini's hand as he left.

# 21

THE following day—the third day of his illness—was Sunday, and its unbearableness for Dandekar grew with each minute. All the families in the tenement were at home. Their combined noise, the sense of their collective presence in the tiers above, acted on him like a giant press, slowly and efficiently flattening him out.

Outside in the courtyard the pump was working away furiously, interspersed with the thud-thud-thud which was of the municipality's making. More water was drawn, consumed, carried up the stairs and slopped over the floors on this one day, it seemed to Dandekar, than in the whole of the rest of the week.

It was worst in the hot weather, when the tap became a magnet for every child in the block, the cement square about it a favored battlefield and playing ground. They were at it now, pelting up and down the clanging iron stairs, splashing and squealing until his whole body and soul became shrill and cantankerous. He knew it was use-less, but twice he lumbered out all flushed and blotchy as he was and one eye no more than a slit, and clouted as many children as he could catch to relieve his feelings. But it did no more than that. Like flies, he thought, lying in the darkened stifling room, arms and legs sprawled wide on the bed and yet with the sweat crawling down each limb. Like flies that there's nothing to be done about ex-cept endure unless you're rich and English as Wilson was, and all that wire mesh in all the windows. But then the heat was terrible—this powerful, bearing-down heat that you felt nothing could make worse, but wire mesh did. He moved restlessly, shifting each limb from the damp hot trough in which it lay to a transiently cool patch, cursing the impatience which had brought down the blind. In its place Sarojini had hung one of her saris—a thick purple calico ten times worse than mesh would have been, for it let in no air at all. But it effectively kept out the light, and it was the light that he found so fiendishly pain-ful.

At twelve Sarojini came in with his tablets and painted over afresh, with a steady hand, the blisters on his face. Then came the eye drops. He trembled when Sarojini put them in, and thinking of what it had all cost he trembled still more, though he felt too ill to ask Sarojini from where the money had come. At one she brought him his meal—rice boiled to a mush, buttermilk, a pale yellow triangle of lime pickle from which all the hot red goodness of chilies had been washed—invalid food from which he turned in disgust.

"Did the doctor say this was all I should have?"

"It does look a bit insipid, doesn't it?" Sarojini said agreeably. "Perhaps if I mixed in a little fried mustard seed with the rice, and perhaps just a small chili, it'll give it a bit more flavor . . . and the buttermilk really is nice, so cooling, just try one spoonful . . ."

She coaxed and wheedled, her head like dark satin near him, and he came to life.

"It's almost—almost like old times," he said a little wistfully, and was immediately sorry he had spoken, for at once constraint fell between them like a shutter. Sarojini's eyes dropped, she picked up the brass tray on which she had arranged his bowls of food, the empty tumbler of buttermilk.

"Would you like some more?"

He shook his head. His appetite was gone. But he had already eaten well, and he slept. The whole tenement slept, struck down by the sun which had converted the tiered concrete boxes into efficient roasting ovens.

Toward evening, near five, Sarojini came to see to him again. She had bathed and put on a clean cotton sari, and despite the heat and the pain that enveloped his mind he knew what she was going to say. Then she said it, looking straight into his eyes, her own clear and overbright as they often were when she looked at him, though more often she did not; and quite suddenly in the strange clarity of his racked state he knew that she was not really seeing him, that often as now, he no longer existed for her, although some mechanical process made it possible for her to face and converse with him rationally, and even to accord him some gentleness.

"I won't be long," she said, "a couple of hours at the most. I'll be back in time for your next medicine, probably before."

"The children—" he began weakly.

"I'll take them with me, of course." She had it all worked out. "Cousin Rajam has been pressing me to bring them along for weeks . . . I'll leave them with her and pick them up on my way back. I won't be long."

He made no more objections; he had not the will to contest anything further. She's gone, he thought hopelessly. In spite of every difficulty—the heat, the children, my illness—she's gone, nothing can hold her. He lay back, inveighing against the illness that kept him prisoner. I should have gone to Chari the same day, he thought. Sastri warned me not to delay. I should have gone to Chari and said—his head was splitting, but he kept at it tenaciously and worked it out—and said, "This man has a hold over my wife, for reasons I need not go into, and you must break this hold because I cannot, I have tried, and tried, and tried—" He was shouting; he realized that from the sudden hush that had descended on the merrymakers in the taproom. "—and failed," he finished in a whisper, "and it is destroying everything I value."

Monday was another gasping-hot day. The whole city sweltered, as the season slowly worked itself up to the climax of the monsoon. Dandekar lay like a log in his room, watching with his one good eye the sleepy crawl of a lizard across the ceiling. Through the window, despite the sari screen, the acres of concrete, came the smell of bruised vegetation, of grass and plants and flowers crushed under the leaden air, the heavy, low-slung sky. Dandekar knew the smell; at least the memory was there, though he could not remember when he had last been conscious of it. He liked the smell; and the liking ran into something deeper, a feeling that he and the earth suffered together and would be reborn together, that they were fragments of a perfect whole. He knew when he was back at work the feeling would not come. It was rare, and elusive, to be treasured while it lasted; and even now while he thought of his office it was gone. All he could think of now was the terrible heat, and the stupidity of the flies that fell like sluggish suicides into the lazy open jaws of the golden gecko on the ceiling.

At high noon, undeterred by heat as she would have been by cyclone and earthquake once her sense of duty was aroused, Rajam came to visit him. So remote was she from his thoughts that he did not recognize her heavy step, otherwise he would have feigned sleep.

"Ah, Cousin Dandekar." She sank down, placing conspicuously in front of her the small pot of home-churned butter she had brought as a gift for the sick. "Your dear wife told me yesterday you had this severe affliction. I came as soon as I could. I would have come sooner, but it's not always easy to get away—"

"It can't be. You shouldn't have troubled."

"But, Cousin, what trouble is it to visit one's relatives when they are ill? It is the least one can do. Is it not well said, 'He who . . .'"

The homily went on. Dandekar wished Sarojini were there to deflect some part of it, but Sarojini had gone to the office, bearing the doctor's certificate that would tell them all he was sick not shamming; and the girls were of course in school; and he could hardly call the maid in, even with the excuse of exhibiting the child, to bear the brunt of Rajam.

"—so I said, I must go and help dear Sarojini and her husband, and the children too, for what," said Rajam, her eyes growing round, "will become of them if harm should befall the parents?"

"They will survive," said Dandekar, "as other orphans do. However I do not intend making orphans of them yet. I am not at death's door."

"No, no, no, Cousin," agreed Rajam vigorously. "Of

course not—you must not even think of such a thing. Although," she lowered her voice, "I must say when I heard it was the pox—"

"The pox? Did Sarojini say that?"

"No, no, Cousin, she called it something else, some newfangled name I didn't catch—and then she went off in such a hurry—to the Swami you know—"

"*I* know."

"But then I got Lakshmi to describe it for me, and I knew it was the pox."

"Yet you came."

"Yes certainly, Cousin. It was my duty to come. I said to myself: Tomorrow, first thing, I'll go and see him. Besides," said Rajam with great frankness, "I had it long ago, when I was newly married, and it cannot attack you twice. But well I remember how much I suffered—the pain, the itching, the headaches, ah me!—so I know exactly what you are going through."

It almost made him feel worse to listen to her. He said sourly, "But you had smallpox. This is not smallpox, as you will see if you care to look. The blisters are all in one small patch."

"Ah yes, I can see that now." Rajam peered and craned. "It is so dark here I did not notice . . . but as you say, it is all on one side." She bent closer, peering and craning. "How strange it should all be on one side."

"And what is so strange about that?"

"Well, Cousin." Rajam's voice was hushed and solemn. "It does not look to me like any ordinary disease."

"What does it look to you like?" He thought, What is she getting at now? He could tell from her voice, her bulging eyes, that there was something, and though it exasperated him he felt impelled to ask.

"It is not for me to say, Cousin, but since you ask"— her voice sank lower still, to the depth of mystery—"it looks to me like the evil eye."

"Like what?"

"Like the evil eye. I know you will not believe me, Cousin—being educated perhaps it is difficult to believe anything—but my Aunt Sita was afflicted in the same way, all on one side like you and one eye closed and blisters bubbling up over that eye and right up between the hair and no one could tell what caused it—not all the doctors—and in the end she went to a priest. Do you know what he found?" Rajam was whispering now. "That it was the evil eye of her neighbor, who coveted the diamond nose screw that she wore."

Evil eye for a nose screw. Really, he thought with anger, *really*. There were many things he believed in, things that were beyond reason, and there were things to which in common prudence he never offered testament either of belief or disbelief. But this—this evidence of trivial physical mischief for preposterous ends—was too much. He wanted to be furious, but he felt too ill, and it was too hot. He gazed at Rajam helplessly, despising her and not caring whether he showed it or not, and she looked back at him with obstinate eyes, willing him to believe but if not, defying him to laugh at her. They were somehow familiar, that look, those eyes, He had the queer sensation that he was looking into his own; and quite suddenly a long-lodged memory returned, and he was back in a hot summer like this but it was night, the end of that wearisome circus in which all had pranced for viceregal benefit, and he and Wilson had gone up to the terrace to recuperate.

Wilson had been human, even in that imperial age when Englishmen were more often gods; and the silence between them was of peace, rather than that wary incommunication which was the best that interspecies transactions usually achieved. Then Wilson said, lost in that great glittering sapphire of night that arched above them, "These splendid Indian skies . . . they make up for almost everything else. They're out of fairy-story books, those stars, too big and bright to be true. . . . Strange, isn't it, to think that they might be worlds like ours, filled with pompous little performers like us . . ."

"Yes, sir," Dandekar's voice was hushed too, caught up in that majesty above them, "and is it not strange also to think that not one of our lives but is shaped by them, that our horoscopes are traced there in those faraway stars though only the few can chart them?"

"Stars? Horoscopes?" Wilson turned abruptly. His words fell cold and cutting as an ax. "Do you really think all that glory was created in order that some measly little priest can mumble in your ear how many brats your wife is hoing to have?"

Dandekar was equally outraged. "Do you think, sir, that in the universe, which is a whole in God's sight, any part could exist without influencing the others? Oceans rise and fall by the moon." He was quivering with indignation. "Are human lives so worthless that the stars will not touch them?"

Wilson did not answer. He surveyed Dandekar helplessly, with that angry open scorn to which Dandekar knew he was subjecting Rajam; and Rajam's eyes were his own of that long-ago night, obstinate and outraged as he gazed defiantly back at the Englishman.

"I can see you are somewhere else." Rajam's practical voice summoned him back to the present. "So I may as well take my leave. Be sure, Cousin, I shall burn camphor in your name every day until the evil is lifted from you, and I shall tell Sarojini to do likewise, she is a sensible, devout girl—"

At last she was gone. He lay back, exhausted but relieved; and at once the lancinating pain began again.

# 22

ON the fourteenth day from the start of his illness Dandekar woke with a sense of well-being. For a few long, quiet minutes he lay still, savoring this feeling which came from different sources to lay a few roses among the thorns his feet now habitually trod.

He was well again; the pain was gone, and more blessed still, the lopsided mess illness had made of his face had subsided into normalcy. He was going back to the office today, resuming a routine which his orderly nature liked, and which could partially make him forget his troubles. And from today he was no longer alone, for today, before noon, he would ask Chari to help him reclaim what was his. Further than that he did not think. His faith in Chari was absolute, and with the decision to enlist his help some of the weight had gone from his shoulders.

Now he lay quietly, looking down with an aching tenderness at Sarojini, sleeping on a mat on the floor beside his bed as she had slept every night since his illness. Her loosely braided hair lay dark and beautiful on the pillow, with only a few discolored strands to show where the silver would later encroach. Both her arms were up and crossed behind her head, giving a lovely line to her breasts which, long months ago, would have made him throb and burn, his whole body maddened until he had held her and taken her and could at last be still. Now he could look at her calmly from another aspect of love, see the flesh flower pale and beautiful under the thin blue cotton she wore without desire, be aware of the body whose every velvet detail he knew without craving vehement renewal. He wanted her back, not merely because he desired her, or to care for the children, or to keep house as she had once done, nor even because without her his world was unpeopled—no; but because above the sum of all these parts was something else, a spiritual ingrowing which made it impossible for him to be whole so long as any part of her was missing. He had not fully realized; had fretted over the dust on the floor, the neglected house, the mounting bills, the tears of his children, the squandering of their treasure, the defections of his body (for his spirit had always been hers)—until at last in the weeks of heat and pain and those stabbing lucid moments he had come to the truth: that he could have borne all or any of these manifestations, providing only she had not withdrawn from him.

Outside—gentle aftermath to the night's storm—a fine feathery rain was falling, soft as the whir of a young bird's wings. It was an interlude, a space to breathe, a few days grace before the next cycle began, and the swelling pressure built slowly up and up until the sky was ruptured. It would be pleasant, he thought, to walk to the office through this rain. To walk, he stressed to himself: from today no more frantic rushing for the bus, no more tardy arrivals, no more tirades from Ghose, no more trouble from Joseph. He frowned a little. Joseph would bring disenchantment to paradise if he could, not through clumsy ignorance or a pugnacious honesty, but because it amused him to watch the results. And Ghose? He stirred uneasily, but before the thought could begin to cripple him he slid out of bed and started to dress.

By the time he was dressed, some part of his earlier well-being was restored—enough to draw comment from Lakshmi.

"You look different today, Father," she observed. "You look nearly happy."

"Do I?" He was startled. All that effort of shamming, whispering, putting a face on it, shown up in its sheer uselessness by this child's matter-of-fact observation. He said stupidly, "Do you think so too, Ramabai?"

Ramabai raised level eyes to his, weighing the matter, fingering the filmy stole about her shoulders that marked her new maturity. It had chastened her, this new state, given her a deep quiet, these long reflective pauses so foreign to her before.

"Not exactly happy," she said at last. "More peaceful—not quite so eaten up."

His disintegration had been plain, then; observed by both his daughters in detachment, silently, and with what injury he would never be able to gauge. He faced the truth, drained the cup to its bitter dregs, yet heard himself saying, in a voice as weightless as wind-blown chaff—words he knew would be gone with the wine: "That's exactly how I did feel, as if hundreds of ants were eating me alive. You should get yourself covered in blisters and you'll soon see what I mean."

He was strapping on his sandals, about to leave, when Sarojini said, turning from the tulasi before which she sat in worship, "It's true—you do look different today."

He very nearly said, eagerly: "Yes, I do feel different, because from today I shall not be alone, from today things are going to be different." But when he looked at her he thought with sudden fright, *How* different will it be? *What* am I about to do to her? He knew he had to stifle these doubts and he did, but not before he had accepted and come to terms with his role in seeking to take from her the support she relied on, to deny her the force from which she drew strength. It is treachery, he said to her silently. Forgive me.

Kannan, the peon, was the first one to see him. He had his dhoti girded up above his knees and was swabbing the steps of the office building, which were awash.

"Oh Dandekar, sir! How good it is that you are back. You are quite well again—fully restored to health?" He beamed and shone with welcome, giving little extra flicks to the area of step that Dandekar's delicate feet must tread. "Now go carefully, sir—never do to break a bone your first day back and this water! Can't get rid of it, no matter I've been here since seven o'clock."

Dandekar nodded and smiled and ran up the steps, dodging the wavelets each swish of the broom sent down. He was reasonably versed in this kind of hospitable repartee, but in no mood for it this morning, particulary with more of it to come. Besides he wanted to be alone for a while before the rest of his colleagues arrived, to get himself resettled and close as far as possible the hiatus of absence.

He had not thought, with so much on his mind, that he would find it easy to concentrate; but to his surprise within a few minutes of opening his files he found himself absorbed in his work. He had never paused to consider whether his work was interesting or not. He did not do so now, but that it had recovered its former dry reality so

far as to engage his attention was enough for a deep satisfaction—unconscious but healing—to well and flow
through his mind.

The pile in the out tray was mounting—he had just
glanced at it with pleasure—when Sastri came in. He was
wearing his monsoon outfit—dhoti, a rainproof bush jacket, and boots instead of sandals. His footsteps had
sounded ominous—those of the well-shod Ghose—and
Dandekar was halfway into his protective shell before he
realized who it was and emerged.

"Sastri, it's you. You made me jump."

"Saw you, my dear fellow." Sastri was as robust as ever,
his voice boomed in the empty room. "Thought it was
Ghose, didn't you? Mustn't let him scare you, my dear
chap. These Northerners, they've got the brawn and the
brashness but when they want brain they've got to come
South, to you and me and Chari, do you know that? It's
a fact—admitted in Delhi. Now don't let me talk about
that, or I shall forget to ask you how you are."

"I'm quite well. Entirely recovered."

"You look well. Weller than you did before you got
ill."

Dandekar said abruptly, "You know we were talking
about Chari—before I got ill. As soon as he comes in I'm
going to ask him to help me."

"Over the Swami?"

"Yes."

Sastri was quiet. He said, "I knew you'd have to, sooner or later."

It was close on nine. Outside they could hear Kannan exchanging greetings with the first of the arriving clerks. Sastri said quickly, "What do you want Chari to do?"

"I want him to help me."

"Of course, there's only one way. By shifting him— running him out of town."

"Yes." Dandekar drew a long breath. "That's if he can."

Sastri shrugged. "Will he want to? That is the question."

"I don't know." Dandekar had grown very quiet too. "But I have to try. I have to fight. It's my life."

"Yes," said Sastri, and he added, raising his voice as the others streamed in, "Exactly what I advised, my dear fellow."

At noon when Dandekar went in, Chari said, raising his voice above school bells and factory whistles, "Come and see me at five. It'll be easier then."

Dandekar went again at five, but for him it was no easier. He stood in front of the desk, trying to remember the formula he had prepared or the speech with which Sastri had primed him, but both were gone; next urging himself to begin somewhere, anywhere, say it and be done, and maddened that the words would not come.

Chari spoke first. He said abruptly, "You're in debt. Up to the neck. The moneylenders are squeezing you and you want me to help."

"No, sir. I would never go to one of them, sir—never."

Dandekar was outraged. People did, of course, fall into the hands of moneylenders, but they were not people like him. He came of a decent family and a respectable class, had been thrifty all his life except in the last few months, and even now in the straits he was in he had never once considered going to a *bania*. What could Chari be thinking of to suggest such a thing? And Chari thought, noting the bright flare of indignation: It's curious how people will hoist some tattered standard of their own and keep it flying through thick and thin, when the rest of the flags have long been lowered. He said gently, "It's not a vice to be short of money. A lot of people are, including you . . . but that's not why you've come to me."

Dandekar flushed. "No, sir. It's my wife. It's not even her, it's the Swami." He had started now, the stark sentences came easily. "She has a growth, she believes he can cure her, she goes to him more and more, she seems to have no strength except what she can get from him, she gives him whatever she can—clothes, food, money—as much as she can lay her hands on. I never know from day to day what she will take next. Whenever she can she leaves everything to go to him—the children, me, our home, everything. These things were her world but she doesn't seem to want any of it any more. All this is hard to bear, going on month after month, sapping away all we have built together . . ." He stopped, his mouth dry, looking away from Chari's bent listening head and beyond the open window to where the rain was softly falling, frail and gray as the finest mull.

". . . very hard to bear," he went on, his voice as light as a leaf. "But the hardest thing of all—I didn't properly realize it until I was ill—he is taking her away from me."

Chari said brusquely, switching on the light to dispel the evening gloom, "Do you mean he sleeps with her?"

"No, sir, he's not that kind of man."

"How do you know?"

"I went to him. Because I thought that."

"And you were wrong?"

"Yes, sir."

"Then what *do* you mean, he's taking her from you? Has your wife left you?"

"She's still with me," said Dandekar, "but it's only the shell. All that's real is left with the Swami. Sometimes when I look at her I know she has even forgotten that I exist. I know in the Swami's world it is not easy to remember—I've been in it, I know the forgetfulness it brings—but I want to exist, to exist for her. I want my world back, my children happy, my floors swept—"

"Is that important too?"

"Yes, yes, yes," he cried. "In the world I'm in it's important, all the small things are important and I know it's small and petty but I'm a small and petty man—I know it but I'm not fit for anything else, I cannot change myself."

"Yet there's more to it than even that," said Chari gently, ashamed to have caused the outburst, this arrival at self-knowledge which human dignity demanded should be done in privacy. "Any servant girl could sweep your floors for you."

"Yes, sir." Dandekar regained some control. "There is more to it than that. My wife is part of me now—I didn't realize it in all the years it has been happening, but I know now that without her I'm not whole. Being incomplete won't kill me—I know that—but it'll take away most of everything that life means to me."

Chari was silent. He had known Dandekar a good many years, recognized and respected his honesty, integrity, rectitude—all those decent if unspectacular qualities of the average unassuming citizen—but now quite suddenly and simply he had broken this ordinary chrysalis and emerged invested with stature and dignity.

Dandekar said, "I begged the Swami to stop seeing her, but it is she who goes to see him and he will not compel her otherwise. I asked him to refuse to see her, but he will not close his doors to anyone in need. If I compelled her

222

she would obey me, she is my wife . . . I could force her to go to the hospital but her spirit is unwilling, it would not allow her body to recover there."

Chari did not even dispute this. In this country the body had long taken second place, forced into that position by a harshness of circumstance which it would hardly have weathered without the sustenance of the spirit; by a harshness of climate, in which a consideration for the body would have been the purest painful folly; and by the teachings of a religion, itself perhaps shaped by these, which sought to turn the eye inward and find there the core of being. If Sarojini wanted to die she would; better to accept that, go on from there, than break one's back attempting to pull up such deep roots. He said bluntly:

"What do you want me to do?"

"Shift him, sir. Have him moved to the next town. She will not follow him there—she will never leave me physically. It will make no difference to him—his reality is not ours, to him his surroundings do not matter."

Shift him. It could be done. The railway police did it every day, shifting homeless loafers and beggars from station platforms and benches, not telling them where to go but simply to go. Administrative officers did it, moving gypsies and vagrants over the borderline out of their jurisdiction. It didn't solve the problem—it was like life, a problem never stated, never solved, dragging on until buried by time and death—but it gave a temporary respite to some harassed cog in the machinery of society. And the people went: gentle, pliable, if you told them to go they went. Even peasants bedded deep in the soil. Tell them that wretched little plot they scratched for a living was wanted for some land scheme or other and they would go, pots and pans in a bundle on the back of a scraggy donkey, their defeated shoulders showing what they felt like, although after sustained haranguing they had agreed it was for their own good.

But the Swami? On what grounds was he to be moved— that he had enticed—spiritually—the wife of a government employee, taking advantage of her sickness to establish a domination over her for material ends of his own? On the facts it sounded the right conclusion—but is it, *is* it? he wondered, gazing at the waiting clerk, hearing again the weary recital of whittled earnings, worry, debt, neglect, sorrow and uncertainty that had reduced a man plump in the pride of fortunate living into this white-faced shadow—turned him into a thinking, suffering being, after smug and happy years of thought-free life. Yet Dandekar himself—injured, bleeding, come at last for help—had no word against the Swami. He was someone who lived on another plane, against whom it was sometimes necessary for those on lesser planes to band; and that was all.

He said at last, "I'll have to go into it. I can't very well take any action until I have."

When Dandekar had gone, a little tremulous from the unburdening, the slight implication of help forthcoming, Chari sat for a long time, brooding. For months now Dandekar had been severely overwrought, and he had not been able to confine these nervous depredations to his home. His work had reflected it in an exasperating series of errors, omissions, delays, sudden flurried asininities which the best will in the world could not overlook; and a government department was not equipped with that kind of good will. Either Dandekar must take a grip on himself, as Ghose had properly said, or Dandekar must go. But what, he thought, is the use of telling people so? They would if they could. It's because they can't that they fall to pieces or come for help.

For help. He stirred restlessly. Without it Dandekar might carry on a few months longer, muddle along as he was doing now, until some irretrievable blunder earned him the sack. Then he would join the ranks of the unemployed, there to perpetuate his troubles. In a way, of course, it was his outlook. The world was filled with people with problems, for all of whom none less than God could feel concern; yet to send a man one knew, however slight the acquaintance, into these unchartable seas was to transform an impersonal bearable helplessness into a crucifying personal responsibility.

There remained the Swami, whose presence in the town he had been aware of and so far, thankfully, been able to ignore. Now, with a mounting irritation against Dandekar for forcing his hand, and some recognition of the cumulative disasters any move from him might loose, he reluctantly accepted the need to investigate the Swami's activities, and to make independent judgment on the facts and opinions his stricken clerk had laid before him.

# 23

CHARI'S instincts had been to look into it himself; but he reasoned that he was too close to the South, born and bred there and its beliefs and acceptances ground into him, to take a detached view of a phenomenon like the Swami. Partly that, and partly he was rushed; and Ghose was deputed.

"Try to find out if this Swami is up to any good or not," he said vaguely, and unfairly, for by what standard was Ghose to judge? Even in this single, particular and individual case there were two opposed views—Dandekar's, and Dandekar's wife's. Chari thought of this, but then he told himself that Ghose would judge by his own standards, and after all that was what he wanted.

Ghose worked energetically and fast. In a few days he had arrived at preliminary conclusions which, he informed Chari, he would go on to verify by further close observation and questioning. "Yes, but try to be as discreet as you can," urged Chari. "We don't want more trouble than we can help."

"Of course," said Ghose, looking down his long pointed nose.

He set to work again, and in under a week a deputation to protest against the questioning of their beloved Swami and his disciples waited upon Chari. He saw them; and in fairness he saw also the second deputation which had come to present a petition of grievance against the Swami. The same day a pledge of support was delivered, signed mostly by the villagers to judge from the thumbprint signatures, whereas the grievances had come mainly from townsmen. The usual pattern, Chari thought, thumbing through a record of the week's interviews: the simple satisfied, and the sophisticated forever disgruntled. He wondered bleakly which was the truer sophistication.

Meanwhile the stream of callers wishing to speak on the one side or the other—in official hearing—was becoming a flood. They came in groups for safety, for added importance; and hardly a day went by without some deputation or other wanting to see him, patient people who sat like timid sparrows on the benches in the corridors outside his office in the hope that the officious bustling peons would eventually usher them in.

Chari could not see them all, of course; but he had devised a random sampling system of his own which often worked, and which now revealed a fair balance between vilification and praise: on one scale, shining testimony of material help and spiritual comfort, of healing, of peace restored; and on the other, tarnished scale, ugly charges of insidious blackmail, extortion, chicanery and seduction.

"Let sleeping dogs lie," Chari quoted grimly to himself. Leave well alone, why prod the cobra's nest? It was too late for wise adages now; the normally sleepy town was awake, vocal, vociferous; and although Chari had known from the first it was difficult country he could not help dwelling on the indiscretions of his deputy.

"*Discreet,*" repeated Ghose, smarting. "I have been, as far as I know how, but I'm not an invisible man. Perhaps you can tell me how to become one."

Despite his cares Chari saw the validity of this. Ghose with his long thin nose and passionate eyes, his height, his intense Northern ways, could hardly go unnoticed in a crowd of short, dark, mild-eyed and mild-mannered Southerners. He had been expecting too much—perhaps the impossible—by supposing Ghose could make inquiries without raising a storm. Yet he was valuable, for if he worked in the glare it was still in detachment, and his opinions would never be shaped and colored by the South.

With a lowering sense of disloyalty to his colleague, Chari began investigations on his own. He went, more or less incognito, to prayer meetings in the whitewashed house on the outskirts of the town; he went to the village settlement, where he was honestly unknown; he went wherever he thought he could hear people talk of the Swami, and he listened to all that was said, but the truth never was—and he recognized that it never could be—absolute. Differing viewpoints produced conflicting evidence, and the most he could do was to position himself as well as he could outside, resolve the conflict fairly on the side of truth. But it was like trying to balance a pair of scales standing on quicksands. As fast as he went, the truth receded faster. Was the Swami a charlatan, or a saint? He could not make up his mind. Heart spoke one way, head the other, and sometimes the two changed places.

Ghose, more fortunate, was not so tormented. He produced quite soon a neat watertight little report on the activities of the Swami, with a recommendation in red at the end for his removal. Appended to the report were two lists showing the Swami's depredations, material and moral. Chari studied them, not without admiration. Ghose had been most thorough; the minutest of details had been carefully entered. On the first list he read:

| | | | |
|---|---|---|---|
| 11 | March | 12 seed pearls | ... gift |
| 15 | " | 1 pair ruby earrings | ... " |
| 18 | " | 1 silver plate | ... " |
| 20 | " | 1 sack rice | ... " |
| 21 | " | 20 tender coconuts | ... " |
| 22 | " | 500 rupees | ... legacy |

The account for three months ran to ten pages. The second list was much shorter; even in their indignation people had been reluctant to parade their private lives.

| 2 March | Threats uttered. | 20 rupees taken. |
| 16 " | Daughter of R.V.S. enticed from father's protection. | |
| 19 " | Wife of S.M. seduced. | |

Chari looked up at this item. "How do you know she was?"

"Seduced? Because her husband told me," said Ghose.

"I meant how did he reach that conclusion?"

"She spent all night with the Swami in his village," said Ghose stiffly. "It's a reasonable assumption."

It was, of course. Yet Dandekar, having drawn a similar inference, had eventually rejected it. Chari frowned, the thread of some elusive clue dragging across and irritating his mind. And then it came to him.

"It would be reasonable," he said, "under ordinary circumstances. But there's no option to staying the night in that village if the ferry isn't plying."

"Well, of course, if one wishes to make excuses," said Ghose with the dark angry blood suffusing his face, "one always can."

That made Chari wince—the germ of truth that could not be blown like the rest of the chaff to the winds, the maggot in the wound touching him on the raw. Deliberately he forbore to rejoin on the instant; waited; then with as much care as had gone into compiling the lists he began examining the details and inferences. Ghose answered briefly, coldly, his mouth set hard and showing two white lines above his compressed lips. I'm goading him, thought Chari wearily, defeating my own ends, moving him to attack when what I want in the name of truth is neutrality. He tried to fashion his words with care, wrenching them into guileless shape, but the questions he had perforce to put did not fit easily into tactful frames, and Ghose's face grew darker as he proceeded, and his voice was honed to a bitter-sharp edge.

He was done at last, and the brash sun of midafternoon beat harshly into the room. The blinds were usually down by this time; the peons must have forgotten or, the sin of interruption well dinned into them, were hanging about somewhere outside in the dazed stupefaction which trumpets would not disrupt. Chari got up stiffly from his chair and let down the blinds, then he said, still at the window and the cords in his hand, "Well? What do you think?"

"You know what I think."

"That he is a fraud, an impostor, a man who preys on the credulous of whom there are so many in the South."

Ghose did not trouble to refute or even pretend to refute this. "Of course," he said contemptuously. "There's no question about it at all. He's an out-and-out impostor, the whole atmosphere just reeks of it."

"What atmosphere?"

"For one thing, the incense he uses. All those joss sticks." Ghose shuddered at the memory. "I almost retched, every time I went to a meeting in that house."

"You would certainly have without," said Chari grimly. "Disease smells pretty high at close range in a packed room."

Ghose's nose wrinkled in distaste. He preferred to remember only the nobility of suffering and dying, forget its squalor; and the raw description vaguely shocked him, it was against good taste—the worst kind of minor offense.

"Maybe," he said. "But you don't use incense to disguise smells."

"Don't you?"

"No, not mainly. You use it mainly for effect, to get people onto that dangerous edge where one tap from you and they topple over into your power."

"It's not so uncommon an adjunct to worship."

"Not worship. Religious mania. No man when he worships alone in his house burns great gobs of resins and camphor and joss sticks."

Chari was silent. He could remember light white ash fluffing away from the burning camphor in the tiny shrine of his family house; the glow of joss sticks. filling the air with a lingering pungency; the frankincense, jagged and amber among coals in the bright silver censer, visibly wasting to nothing as the thick white smoke gushed from its sides like milk. They had worshiped there; or perhaps Ghose was right, it had been induced ecstasy.

"And that extraordinary ménage of his," Ghose burst out again, unable to bear the silence. (Hasn't the guts to come out with it, to say he doesn't agree with me, he raged to himself.) "A collection of grotesques—"

"Grotesques?"

"Well, cripples. But they're not ordinary cripples such as ones sees any day on the streets, the ones he has have to be spectacular, like a side show in a fair. The worst of 'em is that dwarf guarding the place like a watchdog—a showpiece, like those leopards princelings used to keep tied up on the lawn."

It was an apt description and, thought Chari, perhaps a just one. Then slowly the medal turned, as unfortunately it often did, to show the reverse inscription; and he could not help reflecting that the lightly marred could walk the streets unscathed, it was the grotesques who needed shelter.

Ghose, awaiting the pointed comment, the point-blank disagreement which he had told himself was all he could expect, discerned instead a measure of sympathy in Chari's glance and was so surprised that he failed to notice how briefly it had glimmered and gone. He said, more soberly than he had done heretofore, some of the aggressiveness sheared off, "It may be a coincidence, of course, that he seems to get only the worst cases. But have you noticed that the people who go to him are nearly all women, and nearly all women with womb trouble? Women, in fact, already bordering on hysteria. One can't help getting suspicious."

"No. Although that kind of trouble produces the worst kind of fear. Of castration. It's more than a loss of a limb or function. It's a destruction of divinity, the fraction that lives in a woman's body, a desecration and a blasphemy . . . they'd rather die than that."

Again, sympathy flowed between the two men. North and South in other fields might struggle for common ground; yet here, Ghose knew, Chari might as easily have spoken of the women in the hills and valleys of North India, as his own women on these parched Southern plains.

The harmony did not last. Chari had his medal, which remorselessy turned to show him its different faces. He knew it did; he often wished it wouldn't. Ghose bore his cross too, but he did not suspect its presence on his back, or if he had suspected might have named it ambition. He wanted to be equal, he wanted his country to be the equal of any in the West; and being equal excluded even a hint of medievalism. He leaned forward now, and he said with the intensity of his ambition, yet somehow managing controlled speech, "Pictures look different to different people.

I'll tell you what it looks like to me, and what it will look like to the world. Here is a man living in apparent poverty whose storerooms are crammed with food and clothing like an Arabian Nights treasure house—for his destitute dependents, so his lieutenants tell you. Whose claims to spiritual healing make women flock to him, paying for illusory cures in cash and kind and any other way he asks them to. Who deals in an atmosphere of drugs, devils, incense—things," he said in a sudden disgust, "that healthier countries got rid of centuries ago."

"And so?"

"He must go. Dismantle the circus and drum him out of town. He's battening on credulous fools here, living like a lord on the poor and making them poorer, heaven help them! To let him carry on is to make ourselves the laughingstock of the world."

Chari almost smiled. "We're hardly a headline town. We're not likely to make world news."

"But it's symbolic. What happens here is a microcosm of all of India. You can't just dismiss it as a small-town happening."

"Which it is."

"Even if it is."

The younger man's face was set and determined, almost fierce; and Chari thought, very near pity: He's taken it badly, those years of occupation . . . it'll take all his life to straighten out the kinks, and meanwhile there are these ridiculous attitudes to impress the world and prove he's right out in front with the best of the modern bombs and all, but no witches, no holy man; and I must be patient with him, God help me! But patience, pity, both dissolved in irritation. He said shortly, "All right. Get him out. Then we'll take all the sick he leaves behind into our own homes like the good Gandhians we undoubtedly are."

"The sick will go to the right place for them."

"To heaven?"

"To the hospital."

"Which hospital? That ultramodern clinic? They're fanatical on keeping the well well, they're not so keen on patching up the sick."

"I meant the General Hospital."

"The General Hospital," said Chari evenly, "was filled before they finished building it."

"It'll have to take them," said Ghose. "It's an administrative problem. It will be solved."

"Like other administrative problems?"

Ghose flushed. "Room will be found," he repeated obstinately.

"A hundred extra beds? You think so? That is roughly the number the Swami keeps going on faith and hope and other ingredients in dispute."

Even as the problem crystallized in words Chari knew, wearily, that Dandekar had lost. For good and evil together, the Swami would remain.

Ghose's voice cut through the shrinking train of his thoughts.

"You're going to leave him alone. You think he's genuine."

"It doesn't really matter what I think. Or what you think. It's the people that count."

Chari had spoken without calculation, yet he realized, fortuitously, that this notion lay very close to his assistant's heart. Ghose responded at once, shedding thorns and prickles from voice and manner as before.

"Yes, one must think of what the people think . . . they're with him, aren't they, a lot of them? Even I could see that. And you know I felt they were right and he might be genuine—just once, when I was talking to him and he said if I told him to go he would and it didn't matter to him either way but no good would come of it, no good ever came from usurping another's life. I almost believed in him then."

"You don't now."

"No. The evidence against him is too strong. One must be careful not to be overwhelmed by personality."

Chari let it go at that. Perhaps he was so overwhelmed; perhaps those others were too. Briefly he wondered whether to tell Ghose he had decided in spite of all this against moving the Swami. He desisted. The lines of fatigue had deepened on Ghose's face; there would be no harm in letting the matter rest, or the man.

Meanwhile there was Dandekar, whose wish to see the last of the Swami was as great as Ghose's, but for more real, less tortuous reasons.

# 24

DANDEKAR, confident that at last help was near, found himself able to bear with tranquillity the continuing dependence of his wife upon the Swami.

This tranquillity repeated itself, like reflections in some lovely procession of mirrors, passing from him to his wife, to their children, even to the baby and the maid and the rooms in which they lived and so back to him, giving him bitter-sweet glimpses of what life had been like before his troubles began. Sometimes he wondered, frightened, if the whole wretched year had been of his manufacture; whether, if he had commanded this serenity earlier, life might not have presented a more proportioned look in place of that looming prospect that had tormented him. But then, honestly, he recognized that serenity was not at his command and never had been. It was his now because he believed he could see light edging up his horizon; prolong the night, and the frenzy would start.

From the moment of going to him he had had complete faith in Chari; it simply did not enter his mind that he would do nothing. Chari had said he would look into it— he remembered the words clearly, yet his mind had somehow, and firmly, drawn from them a definite assurance of help. When first Ghose, then Chari, instituted inquiries, it affirmed Chari's promise to look into it; when the deputations started, it confirmed his assumption that Chari was taking steps to shift the Swami; and of the rumors that raged through office and town, his selective mind registered only those that spoke of the Swami's impending departure.

"What makes you so sure?" asked Sastri, with a twinge of anxiety for his friend's well-being. He was fully in Dandekar's confidence now, better informed of his affairs than ever he had been, whereas the others, agog with curiosity, had only suspicions and guesswork to go on.

"What is there to make me unsure?" countered Dandekar reasonably.

"They want him out of it," said Joseph, with a side glance at Dandekar. "Ghose is trying hard to get rid of him, so they say in the market place, because the holy man's carried away somebody's wife. But Ghose isn't going to succeed, that's the latest market news. Apparently wives like being carried away by holy men. I speak figuratively of course."

Even then Dandekar was not discomposed. He discounted, briefly, Joseph's latest news, and then quietly dropped the subject.

With the same equanimity he bore the absence of his wife, watched her come and go, more often than not bearing gifts, and retained his calm. What did a few gifts matter, a rupee or two, some measures of rice? He could retrieve it all, and more, once his wife had come back to him, once he had known again those tenuous, unnamable riches wife and home had in them the power to create. Here again, mercifully, his trembling mind pulled another door shut. Sarojini had not been cured. The tumor was quiescent, that was all. If it began eating into her again she would have to go to the hospital and have it cut out of her, and then—then and thereafterwards all would be well, he told himself, so forcibly that other possibilities were blasted to nothing before they could even cast their shadows on his mind.

Since the beginning of the end of his nightmare he had come straight home from the office—no dawdling, no deviation, nothing now, impelled him to either. It gave him more time with his children, and he tried, as best he could, to make up to them for the absences of their mother. Indeed, that he had not done so before was a standing reproach to him, especially when he looked into the dark eyes of his son, disturbed and questioning from a conflict his child's mind had sensed, which apparently a tenderness of years was no bar to sensing although understanding might be.

He was playing with the child one day, modeling small animals from a flour and water dough, when to his surprise he saw Sarojini coming in—much earlier than she did once she had gone out. She looked a little dazed, and she was carrying the platterful of coconuts and mangoes which he had seen neatly laid out the night before in preparation for her visit to the Swami. His stomach turned; this could mean only that the Swami had gone, and although he had been expecting it his centers of feeling began a wild somersaulting that made him a little giddy. Gently, with great care, he slid the child off his lap and shepherding him inside left him with the maid. Then after some hesitation, afraid for the first time in his life of his wife, he forced himself to go back.

Sarojini was still standing listlessly where he had left her; she had not even attempted to go after the boy.

"You're back early?"

"Yes." The sound of his voice seemed to force her to some kind of action. She went to her old place beside his easy chair and sat down, arranging her sari—more from a habit than anything else, for she was obviously beyond such conscious care—in precise folds about her. "The Swami wasn't there. He's gone."

"Gone? Do you mean to his village?"

"No. He's gone for good. He's not told anyone where."

All his instincts forbade it, but he simulated surprise.

"For good? Surely not. This is his home—why should he leave it?"

"Because there were those who wanted him to go," she answered him directly, yet gently enough. "Because his presence caused controversy, and he wanted to end it. And after all he was not like us, he had no attachments to keep him in this or that place . . . it was the people about him that formed an attachment to him though it was against all his teaching."

At that moment, if it had been in Dandekar's power to bring the Swami back, he would have done it. He said wretchedly, "And you?"

"I? What about me?"

"What will you do?"

"Nothing. What should I do? I formed an attachment, it is broken, that is all. One must accept it."

"Do you?"

She said gently, "Of course. It would be sinful to batter oneself to pieces because one refuses to recognize that another's life is his own. If the Swami chose to go, it was his decision. One must accept it in good heart."

"If he didn't choose? If—if the decision was a forced one?"

"Even if that were so."

"Is that what he said?"

"Why do you ask?"

"I must know."

"It was one of the things he said," she answered at last. "He prepared us for his going, I realize that now though I didn't at the time . . . perhaps because I didn't want to. That can happen, you know? Your mind shut it out for your sake?"

"I know," he said, aching. "I know."

"He said there must be no repining," she said. "He was insistent on that."

"It's not easy, not to."

"No. But it's not impossible."

He managed to look at her. Her face was very calm, like her voice. She's learned acceptance from him, he thought, and then, jealousy swooping down like eagles from nowhere to claim him, he thought: Am I to be indebted to this man for giving my wife back to me? The passion burned itself out, as swifty as it had taken fire. No matter, he thought wearily. He took her from me, he has given her back, and that is the heart of the matter.

Hesitantly, with a feeling of strangeness—almost virginity—he took her hands and held them, cherishing them between his own.

"You will be cured. Even without him, even though I know you haven't much faith in hospitals. I know you will."

"I know," she answered. "He said I would be, and not to hold back when the time came. I'm not afraid now of knives or doctors, or what they may do. All will be well. He said so."

Her face was confident, serene. He's achieved the impossible, Dandekar thought, sponged away those fears and memories, driven out her devils. He has done what I couldn't do. So I am to be humbled, beholden once more to this man of all others. Well if I am, he thought, so be it. It was less tiring than to rebel: and, after a while, it became touched with something like peace, like a homecoming.

There was no question of letter or telephone. He had no telephone, they had no time to write. So he waited in a stupor like the others, hour after hour on the hot veranda. When at last they allowed him to see her it was only for a few minutes.

"Yes, yes, she's all right," said the nurse who was trying to hustle him out. "Can't you see for yourself?"

She looked waxen to him, flattened out like a woman after giving birth, and something remote about her like people who are about to die, groping for some meaning, some connection between themselves and the receding world.

"She hasn't come fully out of it yet," said the nurse pityingly.

"Out of what?" he asked stupidly.

"The anesthetic, of course," she answered.

The anesthetic, that explains it, he thought. She has known a brief death, how can I expect her to look ordinary, earth-bound?

"Come on now." The nurse's voice grew firmer, more urgent; she had seen the team of doctors entering the adjoining ward, they would be here in a matter of minutes and here was this simpleton stuck like a bur to the bed. "Can't you see she's asleep?"

"Asleep," said Dandekar, gently touching his wife's smooth forehead. He would have gone then, but the doctors were in the room, the scamper and flurry of their entry roused him from his preoccupation. He looked up, focusing only slowly until he saw Sarojini's doctor in the center of the group—the same woman he had gone to over a year ago, though it seemed like yesterday now that they were face to face—and all his faculties returned. Brushing the nurse aside he made for her, dodging the minions who were converging on him, intent on deflecting this petty human detail from a busy surgeon's life.

"My wife," he said directly. "Is she going to live?"

"Your wife?" The doctor frowned, and instantly a dozen voices had informed her who was meant, the case sheet was efficiently delivered into her hands. "Sarojini, wife of Dandekar . . . yes, she's all right. Didn't the nurse tell you?"

"She did," he said quickly, before the mortified girl could speak. "I wanted to make sure."

"Yes, yes, she's all right," repeated the doctor briskly. "Should be well enough to leave in a week."

This was not strictly true; but the woman could be nursed at home and meanwhile the bed was wanted, more urgently wanted than in any of these last never-endingly urgent years. She moved quickly on.

It's over; at last it's over, he thought. He could hardly walk, his legs were like water reeds, and he sat down in the shade of the nearest tree to recover. It was a banyan, the end of a row of banyans. Great gnarled roots dug into the ground, heavy trusses of root hung from the spreading branches, striving to touch the soil, to earth themselves and begin new life. Some were aerial still, hardly descended; others deeply embedded, thickened into stem and tree trunk. The commonest of trees, scarcely if ever noticed; yet now he was touched by the beauty of that colonnade, the continuing line of sapling and giant. His eye moved slowly down the quiet vista, and he thought: Perhaps my life will be as peaceful too, hereafter. It was the quality he longed for above all.

After a while he got up, feeling physically rested but lost—like an immigrant facing fresh arrival in a new country. Uncertain where to go, he yet began to walk, in a vague hope that the sense of disorientation would lift. Strength had returned to his limbs. He watched his legs swinging his torso along without any direction from him other than the avoidance of obstacles. He did not know where they were taking him; he did not care until, aghast, he realized he was outside the whitewashed house in the narrow street. Then he stopped, and all his senses quivered and sprang into life. He knew he was in danger; he knew he ought to retreat, to walk as rapidly as possible away from this place and never come back. He could not.

In front of the open archway the slatted screen swayed gently, impersonally, neither inviting him to enter nor repulsing him. Why can't I go away? he thought. What is it to do with me? The question was still ringing in his ears as he mounted the steps and swung the screen aside. Beyond was the passage, the long corridor that led to the courtyard. He walked slowly along it in his bare feet, down to the courtyard where a small silent group of people had gathered. They followed him with their eyes as he passed, but they said nothing. They were doing nothing, but it was an arid negation of life, not its peaceful affirmation. In the center of the courtyard where he had seen them worship it stood a tulasi tree, neglected, its leaves shriveled from lack of water, the soil dry and crumbling in the brass. He turned from the tulasi to the faces of the people he passed, and, with a shock, thought he recognized there the same disintegration. Averting his eyes he hurried by as quickly as possible and found himself in one of the larger storerooms.

It was almost empty. The tall grain chests stood open, their lining of tin glinting through the meager layers of rice. Viscid oil, all that was left, barely coated the bottom of the stone jars. On the floor, their mouths open, drawstrings slack, were slumped the sacks once heavy with flour. The cornucopia was dry.

The storerooms interconnected, leading from one to another and so to the veranda. Beyond, he knew, was the staircase to the terrace. I've come so far, he thought, I may as well go on; and slowly he went to the foot of the stairs. He was about to ascend when the voice came, so loud in the silent house that his nerves began to screech.

"Why in the name of the devil have you come here?"

He stood stock-still, while the shock waves traveled over him, partially numbing him. He knew the rasping voice, but he wasn't, yet, able to answer it.

"I said, What are you doing here?" The dwarf emerged from the darkness, squat, ugly, rolling a little on his bowlegs, his yellowish eyes glittering in his squashed face.

"I—was passing." He felt he was suffocating, so tight was his breast. "I had to come in."

"Why?"

"To—to see if the Swami was back."

"He's not back. He'll never be back. You knew that before ever you set foot in this house."

"No," he stammered. "I didn't know—I wasn't sure. If I had been I wouldn't have come."

"Whom are you trying to deceive?" The dwarf spat deliberately, ridding his mouth of the taste of falsehood. "You came because you couldn't help yourself. Your guilt dragged you. You came, because you had to come and see for yourself."

"See what?" cried Dandekar. "What is there to see?"

"The derelict." The dwarf gestured toward the court-yard. "The abandoned, the people—if you can call them that—out there. The Swami used to hold them up, keep their heads above water. He won't come any more. I've told them he never will again—he's gone, and he's never coming back. I've been telling them that twice a day and at last it's begun to sink in. They're going under now. The spirit's snapped, you can see that, can't you? Their bodies will soon be finished too. The coffers are empty. You've done it all for them."

"The poor are everywhere." Dandekar was shaking. It was a violent effort to speak. "For every one he has abandoned there will be another he is succoring somewhere else."

"I know." The dwarf began to grin, rocking with satisfaction on his short stumpy legs. "But that won't comfort you, will it? If you were like the Swami you could take the universal view; but you can't, you're not big enough. You can't see the people somewhere else even if you try twice a day. But you can see the people here, and they're going to be with you for the rest of your life."

"I didn't know what I was doing." Dandekar's voice was a whisper. "I wanted—so little. My wife—I wanted her back, that was all."

"Your wife—that was all? No." The dwarf's eyes filled with contempt. The short malformed body was almost stiff with disdain. He stood erect beside Dandekar, and it was Dandekar who had no stature. "You have forgotten the other things, for which you came here whining and whimpering. I will get them for you."

He went back to the dark well of the stairs and returned with his arms burdened. The silver cups, the water-lily ashtray, the chain from his son's neck—he saw them all for a second before the dwarf, spreading his arms wide, sent them crashing to the floor.

He had only to stoop and pick them up—the treasured possessions that rolled at his feet. He did not. He stared down at them, motionless, and from them back to the dwarf, and the mark of vengeance on the twisted face straightened his body and cleared his mind.

"I wanted these things and I fought for them because they meant a great deal to me," he said steadily. "That is a fragment of the truth. But I fought also for other things

—my wife, myself, my children, and these are the other fragments, of which even you must be aware. You told me, once, why you came here—that your mind might not grow as warped as your body. Remember that, as I shall remember all my life those who are here, derelict."

The sun had moved past four o'cock, its slanting rays gleamed on the fallen, dented silver vessels. Dandekar kicked them gently aside and went out into the street. Ramabai and Lakshmi would be leaving school about now. He smiled a little. He would go and meet them, with the good news about their mother.

## Date Due

| | | | |
|---|---|---|---|
| Se 27 '60 | | | |
| OCT 19 '60 | | | |
| FEB 1 5 '61 | | | |
| MR 27 '68 | | | |
| AG 22 '73 | | | |
| | | | |
| | | | |
| | | | |
| | | | |
| | | | |
| | | | |
| | | | |
| | | | |
| | | | |
| | | | |
| | | | |
| | | | |
| | | | |
| GB | PRINTED | IN U. S. A. | |